Midnight Secrets

By

Ellen Dugan

Other titles by Ellen Dugan

THE LEGACY OF MAGICK SERIES

Legacy Of Magick, Book 1

Secret Of The Rose, Book 2

Message Of The Crow, Book 3

Beneath An Ivy Moon, Book 4

Under The Holly Moon, Book 5

The Hidden Legacy, Book 6

Spells Of The Heart, Book 7

Sugarplums, Spells & Silver Bells, Book 8

Magick & Magnolias, Book 9

Mistletoe & Ivy, Book 10 (Coming 2019)

THE GYPSY CHRONICLES

Gypsy At Heart, Book 1

Gypsy Spirit, Book 2

DAUGHTERS OF MIDNIGHT SERIES

Midnight Gardens, Book 1

Midnight Masquerade, Book 2

Midnight Prophecy, Book 3

Midnight Star, Book 4

Midnight Secrets, Book 5

Midnight Destiny, Book 6 (Coming 2020)

ACKNOWLEDGMENTS

As always, thanks to my family, friends, beta readers,
and editors.
To Ana, welcome to the team!

With appreciation to John Phillip, Terry, Crystal and
finally to Shawna for all the practical information about
paranormal investigations and gadgets.

For my daughter Erin, who supplied me with the more
unusual information about human remains. I must say,
the couple of years that she worked at a funeral home
has really proven to be invaluable to me as an author.

To the memory of Grandpa Gene, who was by his own
admission, quite the ladies man. And finally to my
quietly hilarious father-in-law, Leroy. These two
wonderful men provided the inspiration for the
character of Leroy.

All the secrets of the world worth knowing
are hiding in plain sight.

-Robin Sloan

PROLOGUE

No one ever expects that a small-town librarian would have a secret life. If you glanced at me while I was at work, most likely all you would see is a thirty-year-old, red-haired woman quietly sitting at the reference desk.

Which is exactly what I would *want* you to see.

Not drawing attention to myself does, in fact, make what I do much easier. Blending in and flying under the radar was an essential part of my life, and an asset to my calling. Now when I say, 'calling,' I'm not speaking of my day job as the branch manager of the Ames Crossing Public Library. No indeed.

This is about my *other* job.

A teenage girl approached the reference desk, and I met her eyes and smiled. "May I help you?"

"Hello, Ms. Beaumont. I was wondering—" Her voice broke and she nervously cleared her throat. "Do you have any books on ghosts?"

I smiled. Ghosts and hauntings are a very popular topic locally. "Yes, we do." I stood and smoothed down my dark blue pencil skirt. "Follow me, please."

I walked her over to the non-fiction section and turned down the rows. I didn't bother glancing over my shoulder to see if she was following. Nervous energy was spiking off her and felt like sharp prickles brushing against my back. I paused and indicated a few books to the teen. "These two titles would be good for you to start with. They have basic information about the different types of hauntings."

"Do any of those books tell you how to get rid of a ghost?" she asked.

I nodded. "A few."

"Thank you," she said, and pulled one of the books I'd shown her.

I resisted the urge to pat her on top of her

head, and instead pointed out a table where she could read and left her to it.

I made my way back to the front, stopping to pick up a discarded children's book from the middle of the floor. It hadn't been there a moment ago. Turning my head, I saw a young mother frantically trying to keep up with her toddler who was running amok in the children's section. 'Timothy the Terror' was loose in the library once again.

"Timothy!" His mother's mortified whisper cut through the calm of the library.

Timothy was not quite three years old, and he was tossing books left and right as he worked his way down the stacks. I stopped at the end of the row, folded my arms and waited for him. The toddler was still running full out when he smacked into my legs, rebounded, and ended up on his butt. His rampage had come to a screeching halt.

The book he was carrying bounced off the floor and landed on the pointy toes of my long black boots. "Hello, Timothy." I gave him my firmest librarian's scowl.

"Uh-oh." His eyes were huge as he stared up

at me.

"We do not throw books in the library," I said. "Nor do we run, or act rowdy."

His bottom lip began to tremble.

"Now," I said. "I want you to go back and pick up all the books you knocked to the floor and bring them to me. Quietly."

"Okay." With tears in his eyes, he nodded and turned around to do so.

"I'm sorry," Timothy's mother said. She was heavily pregnant and carrying several fallen books. "He just got over excited."

I took the books from her arms. "Looks like you have your hands full."

She blew her bangs out of her eyes. "So much for me thinking I could pick up a few romances to read."

"We have a display by the checkout counter of newer release romance novels. Why don't you leave Timothy to me, and go pick out a few books for yourself?"

"You'd do that for me?"

"Of course." I smiled and sent her along. When I went back to check on Timothy, he had picked up most of the books and placed them into a neat stack on the carpet.

"I picked the books all up," he said, gravely.

I nodded. "What a good job you've done." I noticed the dinosaur on his sweatshirt and pulled a large picture book off the top shelf. "Here is a book on dinosaurs that I think you'll like."

Timothy accepted the book with a smile. "I like pictures!"

While Timothy grinned over the illustrations, I selected a few more popular picture books and held out my hand to him. "Let's take these up to the checkout counter and you can take them home to read."

"Okay!" Timothy tucked the book under one arm, grabbed my hand, and happily followed me to the front.

After they had checked out, I waved goodbye to the little hellion and his beleaguered mother. *Peace once again reigned in my library, and I hadn't even had to break out any magick,* I thought. *If only all problems with monsters were so easily solved.*

My name is Amanda Beaumont. I live in Ames Crossing, Illinois, where the two largest rivers in North America meet. In this location we have an intersection of several ley lines. These natural conduits of energy attract paranormal phenomena of all types, such as: cryptids, monsters, ghosts, and last but not least, witches.

Because of the latter, I'm bound to an inheritance I never asked for. For my family line has been tasked with keeping the balance between good and evil. While modern-day practitioners such as the Midnight family are locally known for their gentle wise-women practices and herbalism...not all the members of their family were goodness and light.

Several generations ago one individual in the Midnight family was quite dark. She was notorious for working hexes and curses, and her avocation paid quite well. Her name was Louisa Midnight. How can I be so sure of what Louisa did? Because, Louisa Midnight married Eugene Beaumont. They had only one son, Victor, who was born in 1848.

Victor Beaumont was my three times great-grandfather, which meant that *I* was a direct descendant of Louisa Midnight.

Yes, I too am a daughter of Midnight, albeit a secret one.

Over the years, the Beaumont branch of the Midnight family tree was forgotten—and the Beaumonts worked hard to make that happen. My great-grandfather, grandfather, and father have each worked behind the scenes trying to restore the balance and to minimize the damage that Louisa's curses have wrought.

The Beaumonts have become the keepers of a chilling heritage—Louisa's home, property, her personal papers, journals, and spell books. My predecessors had done their best to clean up the energetic chaos that Louisa had left in her wake...And now it's my turn. Today, I am the most recent Guardian of Ames Crossing.

Hence that *other* job I mentioned.

I had been studying, preparing and working my whole life to take over this task from my father. But instead of watching from afar, for the first time in generations, a Beaumont had made contact with our distant relatives, the Midnights.

When the invitation to attend the grand opening of the hotel suites at the Marquette

Mansion had dropped in my lap, I'd taken it. I simply swallowed my distaste for the odious man who'd invited me and went. It was the perfect opportunity to get an up-close look at the mansion, and to learn more about the family that had started all the drama two hundred years ago. It also had granted me the chance to rub elbows *anonymously* with my distant cousins, the Midnights, at the same time.

Unfortunately, the evening hadn't gone quite as I'd envisioned it...

In my mind I would have been much more graceful, poised and powerful. Getting manhandled and knocked on my backside by an over-amorous drunk hadn't been one of the scenarios I'd envisioned. But I should know better than anyone, that fate often has its own plans.

In the end, it was Estella Flores who had come to my aid. She surprised me further by seeking me out later for information *and* revealing that she was part of the Midnight family.

The incident Estella was interested in involved an almost two-hundred-year-old murder mystery. A mystery that still had folks in the village talking about it, and an unsolved crime the Beaumont family—my family—believes was made even worse by Louisa and her dark magick.

I hadn't expected to like her, but Estella was *nothing* like the rest of the current-day Midnight family. She was a feisty Latina, strong, tough and streetwise. That sheen of faery tale enchantment that had blessed her trio of half-sisters hadn't rubbed off on Estella.

Nor had it rubbed off on me.

I tucked a strand of my auburn hair back into the bun I'd worn today. *Apparently the faery tale only applied to the blondes in the family…* I smirked to myself.

The rest of us had to work when it came to magick.

CHAPTER ONE

At five minutes to closing time, it began. The rhythmic growling sound that drifted through the library could best be described with one word: unholy. I whipped my head to the left and discovered the cause. As usual, the source of the disturbance came from the periodical section. Narrowing my eyes, I stood and began to discreetly herd the library patrons farther away from the horrific noise. Once I had everyone safely out the door, I flipped the locks and turned to face my opponent.

This wasn't the first time I had tangled with this particular adversary...our history was long and colorful.

Cautiously, I began my approach from behind. The flames from the gas fireplace created an eerie flickering light that danced across the hardwood floor. It highlighted the face of the source of the disturbance in a demonic shade of red. I braced myself for the coming battle, and swooped in for the kill...

"Gotcha!" I cried, triumphantly.

Leroy Holtgrave, one of my favorite library patrons, jolted awake. "What?" He sat bolt upright in the leather chair.

"You fell asleep again, Leroy," I said.

"I wasn't sleeping," he insisted, as always. "I was only resting my eyes."

"No, sir." I dropped my hand on his shoulder. "You were out cold, and your snoring was loud enough to wake the dead."

"I don't snore. I sort of breathe loud."

"Right." I clicked off the gas flames for the logs. "Be that as it may, it's closing time."

"I was just waiting for you." He rose to his feet. "You shouldn't close up by yourself, Mandy."

I smiled. "I'm perfectly capable."

"I promised your father that I'd keep an eye on his best girl," he said, and shrugged his jacket back on. Leroy and my father had been friends for most of their lives. Since my parents had moved to Florida permanently a few years ago, Leroy haunted the library on a fairly regular basis.

I adored the older man, otherwise I'd never let him get away with calling me *Mandy*. "I appreciate that you do look out for me." With a smile, I firmly steered the seventy-year-old gentleman out the door.

"Go lock up. I'll maintain the area," he said, and was completely serious.

I didn't bother to sigh or roll my eyes, as I knew that he would continue to stand right outside the door, surveying the area and waiting until I switched off the lights, closed up, and let myself out. Quickly, I went through the routine of setting the alarm, locking the door, and waiting until I heard the three beeps signaling that the alarm was set.

"All secure," I told him. Because only then, would Leroy shuffle off to his car.

"Goodnight." He gave me a snappy salute.

I walked toward my own car, buttoning up my jacket against the cool November breeze. I waved goodbye as he pulled his sedan out of the library parking lot.

As soon as Leroy's car had disappeared around the corner, I turned on my heel and instead of getting in my own car, set out across the street heading for *Camilla's Lotions & Potions.*

The traffic was light in the village on a Saturday afternoon. Any tourists were more than likely up at the Marquette property on the cliffs, checking out the winery shop, or perhaps indulging in the new haunted history tours they were offering at the mansion. I crossed the street, my high heeled boots clicking on the pavement, and stepped up on the sidewalk.

Reaching for the shop door, I pulled it open and saw that my friend, Estella Flores Midnight, was ringing up a trio of women. I raised my hand in greeting and ambled toward the back of the store. I decided to browse while the customers finished their purchases. Spying a tester for an all-natural hand lotion, I tested a small dab. I held my fingers to my nose and found the fragrance to be mild. Pleased, I squirted more on my hands and rubbed it in.

Today, Estella had her dark hair in a high

ponytail. She was wearing a black button-down blouse with a work apron tied over that in the shop owner's signature color: pink. She smiled blandly and nodded as the trio of women chattered away. I watched her efficiently wrap bottles in black and white striped tissue and slip their purchases in a pink-handled paper bag the same shade of blush as her apron.

Cheerfully, she herded the women to the door and once they left, she let out a long sigh. "I thought they'd never leave," she said.

I tucked my tongue in my cheek. "Nice apron."

Estella rolled her eyes. "I asked Camilla for a black work shirt so I could avoid wearing the store polo all the time, and what does she do? Goes out and orders *pink* work aprons for us to wear instead!"

I eyeballed the gothic logo on the center of the bib. "At least the lettering is black."

"You don't wanna know what I went through to get her to go with black and white tissue paper for the bags..."

I raised one eyebrow. "Did you put her in a controlled hold and make her kiss the pavement?"

"Damn near." Estella blew a tendril of hair out of her eyes. "Anyway, what's up?"

I shrugged. "I thought I'd drop by and see what you were up to."

"Not a freaking thing," she said. "I close up in an hour and when I go back to the farmhouse, I think Cammy has some project she wants my help with for the wedding. Table numbers, or something."

"A bridesmaid's work is never done."

"I still can't believe she roped me into being a bridesmaid."

"You sound positively thrilled," I said, dryly.

Estella shrugged. "Hey, at least the dress she ordered for me *isn't* pink."

"Jenna's been talking about it non-stop."

"That's right..." Estella said. "You and Jacob's mom work together."

"She's been at the library part-time for a few years now." I smiled. "And by the way, her mother-of-the-groom dress *is* pink, she told me."

"That color is like an epidemic," Estella muttered.

"Regardless, I am looking forward to the wedding."

"I'm looking forward to it too," Estella said. "It's going to be pretty fancy though. And Cammy has these lists of things to do. She has so many damn lists it's scary." Estella crossed herself. "Tonight we're doing table décor."

"Would you like me to rescue you from the dreaded table number project?"

Estella narrowed her eyes. "Don't tease me *chica*. It's been a really long-ass day."

I smiled. "I have some butternut squash soup in the crock pot at home. You could come over for dinner tonight, if you like."

"Yes!" Estella pounced on the invitation. "Cammy was making noises about using glue guns. I burnt the crap out of my fingers the last time I tried working with one."

I adjusted my purple glasses. "Glue guns are one of the many paths to evil."

Estella snorted with laughter. "Well, you'd know, being a Guardian and all."

"Why don't we say you drop by around 5:15?" I said.

"Sure." Estella nodded. "I'll close up at five

and head over to your place."

***

Once I arrived at my house, I switched out my work clothes for a pair of faded old jeans and a comfy sweater. At home in my kitchen, I slid across the floor in thick socks, singing along with the radio. Nyx came prancing in from the living room, leapt to the kitchen counter and meowed along with me.

"We have company for dinner tonight," I said, patting the cat on the top of the head. "What do you think about that?"

In answer, Nyx flipped her tail and sat, keeping a watchful eye as I set the table.

At precisely a quarter after five my back door swung open. On its own. Estella came bounding up the deck steps a few seconds later and walked right in the kitchen.

"*Hola*!" she called out in a cheery voice, and Nyx jumped down and scrambled across the kitchen floor to greet her.

I pulled a loaf of wheat bread I'd been warming out of the oven. "Right on time."

"For the last half hour the store was dead." She unbuttoned her new red winter coat and tossed it on a hook by the back door. "Wow." Estella took a long appreciative sniff. "It smells great in here."

Untouched, the door slowly began to close. Estella, well used to the antics of the house, ignored it.

I noticed a small paper bag in her hands. "What did you bring?"

"Sandalwood rose soap and a jar of honey-oat lotion." Estella placed the bag on the kitchen counter. "You said you were still having trouble with your dry hands." She pulled out a short Mason jar. "I made this lotion myself."

I slid the bread into a napkin-lined basket. "Thanks. My hands get very dried out working at the library. All that paper sucks the moisture right out of them."

"Cammy has been teaching me some of her recipes for lotions and soaps. It's fun to make them, and I get a commission when the stuff *I* made sells at the store. The soap is my own recipe."

"I'll look forward to trying it."

Estella bent over to give the cat some attention. "I noticed you don't wear perfume, and the scent of the sandalwood-rose soap is pretty mild. I think you'll like it."

I was surprised that she'd detected that. "The sandalwood will be useful," I said. "It's very protective, spiritual and great for banishing, while the scent of roses is healing and shields from negativity as well."

Estella straightened. "Exactly. You don't miss a trick. You'll have to let me know what you think of it."

"That honey oatmeal soap you gave me a couple of weeks ago is wonderful. I keep a bar of it at the kitchen sink and in my master bathroom."

"Glad you like it."

I set the basket on the table. "Since I started using it, my hands aren't nearly as cracked as they used to be."

"Can I help with anything?" she asked.

"No, I have it. Go ahead and take a seat."

Estella pulled out a chair at the table while I dished up the soup. I dropped a few croutons on the top and added fresh sprigs of thyme from my garden before serving it.

"Wow, pretty fancy," she said as I placed a bowl in front of her.

I smiled and joined her at the table. "It seemed like just the ticket on a blustery November evening."

"How are things at the library?" Estella asked a few minutes later. "Did you overhear anything new about monsters and ghosts today?"

I sampled the soup for myself. "Nope. It's been quiet for the past week."

"Because Halloween is over?"

"Exactly."

"I am still wrapping my mind around the fact that you get tips while you are at work for your ghost busting—"

I leaned forward, resting my arms on the table. "I am *not* a ghost buster, Estella."

"Okay, monster hunting." She blew on her spoonful of soup. "Demon hunting...whatever you wanna call it."

"Well," I began, "the patrons typically ask me for help with searches for all sorts of information. Haunted houses, local lore, and legend."

"You human search engine, you," Estella teased.

"Right." I nodded. "If anything note worthy comes up, I can move on it discreetly, get an investigation started, and solve the problem before it gets out of hand."

Nyx meowed, as if in agreement.

Estella tipped her head to one side. "Can I ask how your dad gathered his information about spooky stuff back in the day?"

"Dad was the dispatcher for the local Sherriff's department," I said.

"Oh..." Estella put it together. "So he was like in prime position to hear about a paranormal disturbance before anyone else did."

"Exactly." I handed her a piece of the whole wheat bread. "There was a file at the Sherriff's office for any type of paranormal calls...Dad said Sherriff Randal still calls it the 'Weird Files'. Since my father had easy access to that when he worked there, he used it and followed up privately as soon as he was able."

Estella tilted her head as she thought it over.

"What sort of stuff was in the 'Weird Files'?"

I nudged the butter dish closer to her. "Ghosts, paranormal disturbances of all sorts, and of course sightings of the river monster."

Estella's eyebrows went way up. "River monster? Seriously?"

"There are all sorts of local stories about a monster lurking in the depths of the river." I smiled. "We also have the occasional sightings of an overly-large raptor. Every year the Sherriff's department goes and checks out complaints about a mysterious massive bird. A few years ago, a local woman insisted the Piasa bird made off with her Chihuahua."

"Speaking of the Sherriff's department," Estella said, "how's your new boyfriend? Did you two get horizontal yet?"

I fumbled my soup spoon. "Deputy Zakary Parker is fine. Thank you for asking."

"You sounded so prim and proper when you said that."

I smoothed back my hair. "I *am* prim and proper."

Estella pointed at me. "Oh, bullshit. That straight-laced librarian act might have fooled the rest of the village. It doesn't fool me, *chica*."

I lifted one eyebrow. "I'll have you know that my mother raised me to be a lady."

"Yeah?" Estella shot back. "And you told me that your father raised you to kick supernatural ass."

I sniffed. "The two aren't mutually exclusive."

"You're killin' me Smalls." Estella shook her head.

"Ah, *The Sandlot*. Circa 1993." I nodded. "That's an excellent movie."

Estella dropped her head in her hands and laughed. "You are without a doubt the classiest smart-ass I've ever known."

"A small town librarian is expected to look and act a certain way. I need people to see what I want them to..." I paused and took a sip of water. "That, and this very proper hairstyle is a part of my cover."

"Yeah, yeah." Estella waved my argument away. "But you're at home with a friend for the love of god. I mean, doesn't it make your scalp hurt having your hair pulled back so tightly all damn day?"

I nodded. "Sometimes it does."

Estella reached over and snatched a pin from my hair. "Let your hair down, girlfriend. Be yourself!"

I suppose she did have a point. With a shrug, I reached up and pulled the pins out of my bun. With one good shake of my head my auburn hair tumbled down past my shoulders. I sighed in relief.

"I think this is only the second time I've seen you with your hair down," Estella said. "Literally."

I couldn't help but chuckle at her astonished expression.

"Has Zak ever seen you like this?" She wanted to know.

"Of course not. We've only been dating for a month."

I could hardly afford to 'let my hair down' as Estella put it, I knew. *Because if I did, and things ended up in the bedroom, Zak would be bound to see all of the protective symbols tattooed across my back...*I hesitated to mention that fact to my guest. She was only starting to understand what my role as a Guardian entailed. That and she was, after all, still new to the world of magick.

"Well, if you ever decide you want to seduce him," Estella said, giving me a friendly elbow nudge, "wear your hair down and put on something low-cut. Maybe add some dark red lipstick. He'd be a dead man."

I grinned. "I'll be sure and keep that in mind."

Estella ignored her meal and continued to study me. "You honestly look like a completely different person."

"I am still the same," I said. "I assure you."

"I didn't even know that you owned a pair of jeans," Estella said.

"I have sturdy work boots too. I use them when I garden, or hike through the woods searching for—"

"Monsters and evil spirits?" Estella asked.

The hopefulness in her voice made me smile. "I tend to wear all black while I'm doing paranormal investigating, or hunting."

"Shut. Up!" Estella said.

"I don't dress like a librarian all the time." I

wiggled my eyebrows. "For example, I have an all leather outfit that I save for missions where I need to be especially discreet."

"How in the holy hell is a black leather outfit discreet?"

"It blends into the night, and the leather has protected my skin on more than one occasion."

Estella's eyes were huge. "Are you serious?"

"About the leather outfit?" I asked. "Yes, I am. It's quite practical."

Estella leaned forward. "Wow, you have this whole Selena Kyle/ Catwoman thing going on. It's like you have a double life or something."

I studied her carefully. "That's exactly what it is. A double life. Outside of my immediate family and one assistant you are the only one who knows."

"Wait, you have a sidekick?"

I rolled my eyes. "I'd *never* use that term. They're more like family, actually."

"Well I *am* family and your secret is safe with me." She waited a beat. "Catwoman."

I smiled and nodded. "I am glad we're friends, Estella. It's nice to have another woman to talk to and confide in."

"I got your back, *chica.*" Estella patted my shoulder. "Also, I wanna see that leather outfit right after supper."

I started to chuckle. "I think that can be arranged."

***

Since I had Sunday off, I slept in and made myself brunch. After tidying up the kitchen I put my jeans back on, tossed an old sweater over my long-sleeved t-shirt, and laced up my work boots. I twisted my hair up and secured it with a clip to keep it out of the way, I had a side lawn full of leaves to rake.

While I worked in the yard, Nyx sat on the deck steps to oversee the work and promptly stretched out in the sunshine to take a nap. I dumped the last of the pile I'd raked into a leaf bag and stopped for a few moments. Lifting my head, I inhaled deep, enjoying the cozy fragrance of decaying leaves and the smoke from the neighbor's chimney. *There's something magickal about a chilly afternoon in mid-November,* I thought to myself.

With a contented sigh, I rolled up the bag and picked it up. I hauled the leaf bag to the end of my driveway and set it down next to the other four I'd filled.

The Sherriff's cruiser pulled smoothly up to my curb. The driver's window came down and Deputy Zackary Parker leaned his head out. "Hello, gorgeous," he said, slipping off his mirrored sunglasses.

When he smiled, the edges of his blue eyes crinkled, and I had to remind myself *not* to sigh over him like a teenager. "Deputy." I gave him a polite nod instead. "What brings you to my door—curb?"

He looked wonderful in his uniform and heavy brown jacket. He truly was the classic boy-next-door sort of handsome. But it was the blue eyes, broad shoulders and trim hips that upped the ante...

"You know, we've only been dating for a month," he said, "but I think, this is the first time I've seen you in jeans."

I brushed at my clothes. "They're very serviceable. It's somewhat difficult raking leaves in a pencil skirt and boots with three-inch heels."

"You look good in those jeans." His tone of voice was low and appreciative. The look he gave me had me considering him.

"Aren't you on duty?" I asked, lifting a hand to the messy twist of hair at the back of my head. With a quick move I secured the clip to keep my hair under control.

"My shift ends in an hour." He smiled up at me and my heart skipped a beat. "I was wondering if you'd like to go to dinner tonight."

When I didn't answer him immediately he said, "Or we could have dinner at your place, if you prefer."

I felt a twinge of regret at not being able to casually invite him to supper. A normal woman would be able to invite the man she was seeing into her home for dinner, but I couldn't do that. I had absolutely no idea how the house would react to having a stranger inside.

I smiled, and hoped it read as casual and effortless. "I'd enjoy going out to dinner. What did you have in mind?"

His smile grew wider. "Actually, they are

serving dinner up at the Marquette Mansion tonight. It comes with a complimentary wine tasting, a talk about the history of the property, and a tour of the new suites."

"When did they start doing that?"

"This will be the first time. It's something they are trying, wondering if it will encourage more business at the mansion."

I nodded. "Oh, I see."

"Philippe Marquette gave me a couple of tickets for tonight as a way to say thanks for helping out with the grand opening last month."

The 'helping out' he was referring to was most likely when he had to remove a man from the premises—my date, unfortunately—for a drunk and disorderly. I couldn't believe it had only been a month since I'd filed a formal complaint against the sad individual who'd manhandled me at the Marquette Hotel grand opening.

Nevertheless, it had led to me meeting Zakary. Not exactly romantic meeting a man at the Sheriff's station, while filling out paperwork...but fate is often tricky that way.

"That sounds lovely," I said, my mind racing

over the possibilities. This was the perfect opportunity to gather more information on the Marquette family and the house itself. "What time were you thinking?"

"Six thirty?"

"Perfect." I nodded. "I'll be ready."

He reached out a hand to me and I took it. "If I wasn't on duty, I'd climb out of this car and kiss you."

My heart thudded against my ribs. *If I was anyone else,* I thought. *I'd drag you inside and spend the evening going crazy over you...dinner be damned.* But of course, I couldn't say that to him. Instead of revealing my true desires, I settled for saying, "If you weren't on duty, Deputy, I'd let you kiss me."

When he grinned at that, I worked hard to keep a sweet smile on my face. The deputy was driving me crazy. I was beginning to feel like some hormonal teen whenever I was around him. It was most distracting.

He gave my fingers a warm squeeze. "See you tonight."

I let go of his hand and stepped back. "See you."

He put the car in gear, gave me a wave, and pulled away from the curb. I noticed my neighbor across the street, Mrs. Prideaux, was peeking out her front windows.

Old busybody, I thought, and gave her a friendly wave.

The curtains immediately dropped closed.

Amused, I gathered up the rake and the unused leaf bags. I had a couple hours to get ready for my impromptu date, and I wanted to be prepared for anything.

Anything paranormal, that is.

CHAPTER TWO

I was back at the Marquette Mansion, once again as a guest for an event. This time however, my date was infinitely more attractive and a gentleman.

I enjoyed our dinner of prime rib, admiring Deputy Parker as he sat across the table from me. His light brown hair was cut short on the sides, but was long enough at the crown that it tumbled the slightest bit onto his forehead. He was clean shaven—which was more of a job requirement than a fashion choice. There was a long-standing department policy with the Sherriff's office against facial hair.

I sat and listened with enjoyment as Zakary described his afternoon which had included a disturbance at the local antique store, rescuing a kitten who'd been stuck up in a tree, and writing a speeding ticket for the mayor, who'd actually tried to weasel his way out of it.

"Well," I said, "even if the mayor didn't appreciate you doing your job, I'm sure that the Travis sisters were thankful that you rescued their cat."

"The girls let their kitten outside and before they could catch her, she shimmied right up the elm tree in their yard."

The Travis twins were eight years old, and frequent visitors to the library. They were adorable, but quite the handful. "Perhaps I'll recommend a few books on cat training the next time the girls drop by the library."

Zakary chuckled at my dry comment, and when he smiled I felt a jolt all the way to my toes. I'd never considered blue to be a warm color before, but his eyes were an earnest shade of gray-blue. There was something...*cozy* about them.

He was very attractive, and it had been some time since a man had been genuinely interested in me. *Even if he didn't know who the 'real' me truly was.* I caught my train of thought and sighed against the limitations of my public persona.

"You look great tonight," Zakary said.

I lifted a hand to the ivory blouse I wore. It was satiny, with a bow that tied at my throat. I'd paired it with a navy-blue blazer, dressy slacks, and short, tan ankle boots. "Thank you." I smiled, politely. "You look very nice as well."

"Any excuse to bust out my one good suit," he teased.

It should have been a wonderful evening, and a romantic one. Candlelight, good food, wine, and an intimate atmosphere. But I held myself tight and concentrated on playing my role—the buttoned up, soft spoken librarian. For the first time in a long time...I found that it made me miserable.

I studied the man across the table and tried not to let the guilt smother me. Zakary was doing his best to gently woo the woman he *thought* he knew. It was obvious that he believed me to be sheltered and reserved. With a start, I realized he was still speaking, and I tuned back in time to catch the last of his sentence.

"...was lucky enough to be the guy you spoke to when you came in to file your complaint." He grinned. "Otherwise I would have had to let my library books be overdue to find a decent excuse to talk to you."

"You were very kind the day you took my statement," I said. *Even if playing a helpless female had wounded my pride.* I tried not to let that annoyance show, and lifted my wine glass to take a sip. "I'm grateful you were there to help me."

He frowned. "You're not uncomfortable being back at the mansion, are you?"

"I'm absolutely fine, Zakary." I set my glass down. "This has been a lovely evening so far."

"The ghost tour isn't making you anxious, is it?" He reached across the table and rested his fingertips on the back of my hand.

Did he have to be so wonderful? The sincerity simply shimmered off him. I lifted my eyes to his. "No, of course I'm not anxious."

"You'll be safe with me, Amanda," he said earnestly.

"I think the ghost tour will be very informative," I said lightly. "With nearby Alton being labeled as one of the most haunted places in America, we have a permanent display at the library set up on local hauntings, paranormal research and investigations. It's a very popular subject with the patrons."

"I should have realized that you would know all about that."

I recalled what Estella had said. "A human search engine, that's me."

He rubbed his thumb over my wrist. "I'm glad you're looking forward to it, and aren't afraid."

"From what I understand, the house is thought to have a residual style haunting, not an interactive one." It was a safe reply, as it was fairly common knowledge in the village that the mansion was considered haunted.

"So a lower level creep factor." He met my eyes. "Here I was hoping the ghost tour would give you a reason to hold on to me."

It took everything I had to smile. Zakary Parker had no clue that the woman he was sitting across the table from carried a silver athame, several vials of potions, and had a small bottle of holy water in her purse. Not to mention the pair of brass knuckles inscribed with protective glyphs in my blazer pocket.

No, he had no reason at all to suspect or guess at my other avocation.

The truth was, I had banished dozens of ghosts over the years, and solved more than my share of poltergeist problems. I'd also removed a thoroughly evil entity—what most laypeople would've considered a demon—from an old abandoned church. Meaning, a historic house tour in a location considered to be haunted, was child's play.

The sacred tattoos across my back prickled, but not in a warning, more like guilt. The situation was both funny and sad all at the same time. Zakary Parker was a good man. He was charming, funny and sexy, patient, kind and thoughtful. This was a man who volunteered by coaching little league during the summer months. He even was a part-time basketball coach at the local high school. That innate goodness made him even more attractive in my eyes.

When his hand covered mine, I had a sudden flash of insight. Zakary had incorrectly assumed that I was a virgin. Which is why he was being especially patient and gentle with me. We'd been seeing each other for a month and he'd never once pressured me, or even suggested that we take our relationship to the next level. He'd been courting me. Deputy Zakary Parker was so damn sweet, and I was anything but.

I truly didn't deserve him, but I also didn't want to lose him. Men of his caliber didn't come along every day. It'd be wonderful if I could simply be the woman he thought I was. But I wasn't. Feeling slightly ill at the subterfuge, I turned my hand over and gave his hand a squeeze anyway.

He smiled in reaction, and I let go and picked up my knife and fork to finish my dinner. I felt slightly better with a bit of distance between us. Not because I didn't want him to touch me...The truth was, I was *dying* to get my hands on him.

I cleared my throat delicately and made sure my voice would be calm and cool and didn't betray the turmoil that was raging within. "It seems to me, Zakary," I said, lightly. "That you are looking for an excuse to have someone hold onto *you* during the ghost tour. Are you afraid of paranormal perhaps?"

He grinned. "Maybe."

"I'll protect you," I said solemnly.

"You're going to ruin my reputation, Amanda," he teased.

Gods, I'd really like to! I thought. For a moment I wondered what he'd do if I leaned across the table and whispered what I had imagined doing with him.

To him.

All night long.

But the persona I'd worked so hard to establish—that woman—she would *never* lean across the table and whisper a naughty suggestion to her date that they go sneak off somewhere in that old house and have wild, spontaneous, inappropriate, crazy sex.

Right. Now.

With an effort, I reigned it all back in. "*For gods sake Amanda! I* thought. *Pull yourself together!* "Would you excuse me for a moment?" I asked and stood.

He rose to his feet, a concerned look on his

face.

"I'll be right back," I said, scooping up my leather handbag. "I need to visit the ladies' room." I flashed a little smile, quickly walked out of the dining room and into the main hall of the public side of the building, silently lecturing myself the entire way.

Idiot! This was hardly the time to be distracted by a man...even if he was wonderfully sweet. And sexy. I pushed my shoulders back in an effort to remind myself of who and what I was. *Focus, girl. You need to use this opportunity for recon, to gather information. You might be able to help Estella get a handle on the ghosts who'd been picking on her since she moved to Ames Crossing.*

Following the signs to the restrooms, I walked down the hall and came up short when I saw that the museum room that the Marquettes had set up was open. I shot a quick check over my shoulder, saw no one, and stepped inside.

My attention was immediately drawn to the portrait of Pierre-Michel Marquette. The doomed lover of Victoria Midnight and possible murderer of his wife, Bridgette Ames. Looking up at the handsome young face in the portrait made my stomach roil—that and the large auric field that radiated out from the painting had the sacred glyphs on my back flaring to life.

"So you're the one who jumped a ride on Chauncey Marquette..." I murmured.

The longer I studied the painting the more my emotions pulled at me. The resemblance to the current Marquette brother was fascinating. Estella had been right about that. I fought to stay neutral and dispassionate as I viewed the portrait, but it was difficult. Everything she'd told me about her visions and dreams of the man from the 1840's with his lover Victoria, ran through my mind.

I shook off my reaction, and pulled my cell out of my purse. Quickly, I took a couple photos of the portrait. Following my gut, I scanned the area and wondered if anything else in the museum had held onto any energy, negative or otherwise.

The room felt "crowded" even though I was alone. Which meant that paranormal energy was definitely present. Most likely from the residual style haunt, or from a psychic attachment still covering one of the objects in the display cases.

Knowing I needed to return to Zakary soon, I stepped back in the doorway. Clicking the aura photography app on my phone, I backed up to take a wide shot of the entire room. While the app wasn't perfect, it was nice to have a backup to what my own senses told me.

I checked the screen and my stomach jumped. There was indeed a huge auric field around the portrait. I lifted the phone again, zoomed in on the painting and took a second picture. The colors coming off the portrait were all blues, and purple. I'd never seen anything like it before.

There was a spirit attachment to the painting, no doubt. Beyond the obvious aura photo, the uneasy reactions it caused in people was double the confirmation. I heard someone walking down the hall, and had to leave. Slipping the phone back in my purse, I started back the way I came.

After our dinner, Zakary, myself and five other couples were given a tour of the western wing of the mansion. Now that the renovations were complete, there were several suites available for guests on the second and third floors of the mansion. Our tour guide was Camilla Midnight, and I listened very carefully as she gave a quick talk on the history of the house and the most recent paranormal activity surrounding the discovery of the missing Ames family dowry.

It was interesting hearing about it from her first-hand experiences. Although the information wasn't anything I hadn't read in the papers, learned from the folks talking in the library, or from her sister, Estella. I smiled and shook her hand after the tour was over. And wasn't surprised at all that the casual clasping of hands had all the arcane symbols on my back flaring to life.

Camilla Midnight had *power.* I let my eyes go unfocused as she spoke to another attendee and saw that her aura was clear and bright. When it came to people—living people—it wasn't difficult to read auras. I wasn't surprised at all that it appeared to shine around her in a bright rosy pink—not unlike her hair color.

A pink aura often represented a practitioner

who had balanced emotions and a strong link to the divine feminine. It also showed me that she was happily in love and well loved in return. The discovery made me feel better about Estella spending so much time with her half-sister. Estella was smart, but very much a novice when it came to magick. It was a comfort to have Camilla's innate goodness confirmed.

After the tour was completed, Zakary drove me home. He walked me up the steps and across my back deck, stopping outside the kitchen door. It didn't take a psychic to know that he was hoping I would invite him inside. But that couldn't happen, for a myriad of reasons.

Knowing he would take this as confirmation of what he assumed was my virgin status, I inwardly sighed and gave his hand a gentle squeeze. "Thank you for a lovely evening, Zakary."

"You're welcome," he said, and gently pulled me into his arms to kiss me goodnight.

Feeling frustrated by the role I was forced to play, I kissed him back with more heat than I'd originally intended. I felt his response as we stood, wrapped in each other's arms, and I let myself forget, if only for a moment, my responsibilities and my heritage.

The deputy had wound me up more than I realized, and I tugged him closer. He gave a soft grunt of surprise when he landed against me. His kisses began to cruise across my face, and I tilted my head back to encourage him to work his way down my throat.

My heart was pounding, and I fought to stay in control of my own desires. When he brushed his hands gently over my breasts, I could swear I saw stars, and it was glorious.

I wanted him so much! There had to be a way to be with him...

My thoughts came to a screeching halt when I saw movement in the window. I jolted, hard. Someone was inside my house.

As I watched, the curtain twitched aside and a familiar face scowled out at me from inside my own kitchen.

Zakary stopped. He had obviously interpreted my reaction to the discovery as reluctance, and he pulled back. "I'm sorry," he apologized. "I moved too fast for you."

From over his shoulder I could see my uninvited guest rolling their eyes and making exaggerated kissy faces through the glass.

With no other choice, I dropped my eyes to the deck. It was a calculated move to hide my anger at the interruption, but I also knew it would make me appear to be emotionally overwhelmed. "Thank you again, for a lovely evening." I stepped completely back out of his arms, and felt like the world's biggest ass.

"I'll call you tomorrow?" he asked cautiously.

"I'd like that." I made myself meet his eyes. "Goodnight, Zakary." I reached without looking for the door, opened it, and stepped inside, immediately shutting the door behind me.

Even before I could slap the lights on in my kitchen, I smelled the coffee and knew my 'guest' had made themselves right at home.

"Didn't know you were dating the Parker boy, Mandy," a gravelly voice sounded.

"Leroy!" I hit the lights and found him leaning against my kitchen island, ankles crossed, with a mug of coffee in hand. "What in the hell are you doing here?"

"We have ourselves a situation," he said.

I yanked my sexual frustration in line and tossed my purse on the island. "This better be damn good to have you interrupt my evening."

The older man rolled his hazel eyes. "You know I wouldn't show up like this unless it was important."

And he wouldn't. Leroy had assisted my grandfather and my father on investigations for longer than I'd been alive. He'd been my grandpa's right hand, and had been actively involved in both my father's *and* my own training. I respected him almost as much as he drove me crazy.

"What's in the wind?" I crossed my arms and continued to scowl at him. It was acutely embarrassing to have someone who was for all intents and purposes, a second grandfather, watch you kiss your date goodnight.

"We have confirmed poltergeist activity at the antique store."

"Then duty calls," I said with a sigh. I rolled my shoulders against the tension gathered there and made an effort to put my date with Zakary out of my mind.

Leroy set his mug aside, pulled the newest model iPhone from his jacket pocket, and selected his text message icon. I saw that he'd been sent a video, and he tapped on it, and silently handed me the phone.

The video showed a store checkout counter, and the sign above announced it to be *Riverside Antiques*. "Is this security camera footage?" I asked.

"Yes. Mabel Hawkins contacted me this afternoon," he said. "They've been having some disturbances at the antique store for a week or so, and assumed it was malicious mischief. Mabel figured some townies had broken in and played a prank. So I helped them pull the security footage this afternoon, and we found this."

As I watched, several objects went sailing through the air. Plates were tossed from a hutch and shattered on the floor—as if on their own. "Level three, haunting," I murmured.

"I encouraged them to contact the Sherriff's department and file a damage report," Leroy said. "Mabel agreed to keep the nature of the recording between us. Dunno how the current young bucks at the Sheriff's office would take a paranormal problem."

I lifted my gaze from the iPhone's screen. "Zakary told me that he'd taken a call there today." *A disturbance at the antique store, he'd said*, I remembered.

"Where were you two tonight?"

"He took me to dinner up at the Marquette mansion." I handed back his phone.

Leroy nodded. "Good. Did you get a chance to learn anything useful?"

"I did." I pulled my own cell phone out from my bag, punched up the photos, and handed it over.

He whistled under his breath. "Whoo-ee! Look at the auric field around that portrait! What I wouldn't give to get an infrared camera up there."

"Call it a hunch, but I don't think the haunting at the Marquette mansion is going away anytime soon. Considering all the recent restorations to the western wing, it's bound to ramp up."

"That's usually a sure-fire way to piss off

ghosts," Leroy said. "Renovations, and so forth."

"That house is *still* a hot spot." I agreed.

"Speaking of hot spots...How long have you and the deputy been sucking face?" Leroy asked, completely seriously.

I snatched my phone back. "I refuse to dignify that with an answer."

He grinned and wiggled his beetled brows. "Sorry to have interrupted your evening, Mandy, but the activity at the antique store has been ramping up for the past few weeks."

"Since Samhain, when the veil between the world of the living and the dead is thin." I nodded. "Makes sense."

"Mabel is worried that it's only going to get worse," he said.

"Antique stores are often filled with haunted objects..." I began. "It's an environment rife with psychic attachments, and problems caused from negative energies."

Leroy nodded. "Which is why I try to *never* go in the damn places."

"They're not my favorite locations either." I sighed. "Do we have clearance from the owners to go in tonight and investigate?"

"We do. Mabel was *very* grateful that we could get to her right away."

I considered him as he stood there in his jeans, black sweater, and brown suede jacket. He was still dapper even in his seventies, and was looking way too proud of himself. "The widow was grateful, eh?" I poked him in the shoulder. "That's not exactly professional behavior, dating a client."

Leroy straightened. "I'll have you know, I'm considered quite the eligible bachelor at the senior center. I have to fight the ladies off with a stick!" he said, and began to pantomime hand-to-hand combat.

I bit down hard on my lip to keep from laughing. "Let me gear up. Then we can head out and see what we can do to clear this up for Mrs. Hawkins."

"Don't worry, I'll drive!" Leroy cheerfully volunteered.

I didn't bother to roll my eyes. Instead I hustled up the stairs to get changed.

CHAPTER THREE

Leroy's car was a non-descript beige sedan. It resembled a dozen other late model cars, which was why I allowed him to drive. He expertly navigated out of the village and back onto the highway proper. While we drove over to the antique store, Leroy filled me in on everything that had been happening at the shop.

It started when an employee had noticed a woman standing in the store after closing time. She'd walked back to inform the customer that they were closing, and the woman had disappeared. The employee searched everywhere for her, even checking the bathrooms, but found no one. Figuring she was over-tired, the employee had simply shrugged it off.

Until the same scenario began happening every night, with every employee that worked there. During the next week, items were found rearranged in the morning, and no one knew how they were being moved. That had led Mabel's daughter to installing surveillance cameras throughout the store. Now the employees could be at the front counter ringing someone up and view the entire store simultaneously. But they still hadn't been able to figure out what was happening or why, and unfortunately the disturbances had only gotten worse.

"Mabel lost a valued employee last week," Leroy said as he drove along. "Poor Trudy heard a woman crying, but was alone in the store at the time. It spooked her so badly that she grabbed her purse and ran out of the store. She called Mabel from the parking lot behind the shop."

I finished braiding my hair back from my face. It was best to have it out of the way during an investigation. "Did she describe the sound she heard as sad crying or angry wailing?" I asked.

"Unclear," Leroy said as he shrugged. "But according to Mabel, Trudy was pretty upset. She told Mabel to call a priest, and Mabel had to finish her employee's shift because Trudy refused to go back in the store."

"Do we know Trudy's last name?"

"Willis," Leroy supplied. "Trudy Willis."

I thought that over. I knew Trudy Willis. The woman read true crime books and grisly murder mysteries. She was in her forties, and as down-to-earth as they came. "She's a patron at the library. She doesn't strike me as the type to be easily frightened."

"Mabel was disappointed to lose her," he said. "Trudy had worked there for a couple of years."

I thought that over as we arrived at our destination. At nine o'clock on a Sunday night traffic was almost non-existent in Grafton. Leroy killed the headlights and pulled up to the rear entrance of the antique store. He parked and cut the engine.

I glanced over at him. "Ready?"

"I was born ready," he quipped, and opened the car door.

I climbed out of the car and zipped up my leather jacket. The motorcycle jacket was understated and free from shiny trim and buckles. It had thin panels of stretchy fabric along the sides and under the arms. Those strips allowed me freedom of movement, and best of all the black jacket allowed me to go unseen when I needed to blend into the darkness.

The pants I wore were also designed for motorcycle riders. Mostly leather, they were silent as I walked and gave when I needed to move, or climb, or sometimes, run. My shoes were silent and practical low-heeled boots, with a steel toe.

I supposed Estella would be crushed that I wasn't teetering along in four-inch heeled dress boots like some silly heroine on a television show. But the thought of investigating in that sort of footwear was ridiculous. I needed comfort *and* the ability to move quietly. I checked our surroundings and nodded to myself when I saw that there were no security cameras behind the shop. It was quiet and we were unobserved.

Leroy popped the trunk and pulled out his

equipment bag. The man was a retired engineer and a technology junkie. For as long as I could remember he'd always had the latest and greatest 'gizmos'—as he called them—be it a digital camera, audio recorder, cell phone, or computer.

Leroy went to the shop's back door, punched in the security code for me, and held it open. I eased my way inside and waited while he shut the door and locked it behind us. Only the security lights were lit out on the sales floor. While the room and its contents were visible, the light was more shadowy than bright. That suited me just fine. The last thing I wanted or needed was all the store lights to be on, attracting attention from any passersby.

Leroy checked the surveillance video that played on a small monitor in the back room, and shut it down. Neither of us wanted any of our investigating to be recorded for a mundane. Once he pulled the cables, he took out his own mini body camera, clipped it to the front of his jacket and pulled a compact thermal imaging camera free from his satchel. "I'll take a preliminary scan of the space and see if we get any hits," he said.

I was handed the small audio recorder that he used for electronic voice phenomenon or EVPs. It was, truthfully, about the only part of equipment he would allow me to handle. Together, we moved out of the back room and into the storefront proper. Leroy and I had a routine for these sorts of investigations. He was tech, I was magickal security and, if need be, exterminator.

I started the recorder, noting the date and time, and set it down on the front counter. I gave him a nod and off he went, moving through the space. I stayed slightly behind him and far enough back that I wouldn't interfere with his equipment. Yet I was still close enough to protect him if necessary.

I had my own way of sensing the area, and more often than not it was as accurate, if not more so, than any thermal camera. I blew out a long quiet breath, grounded my energy and opened my third eye, allowing myself to 'see' the store with my clairvoyance.

Leroy slowly panned from one side of the store to the other with the thermal imaging camera, while I scanned it energetically. There were dozens of booths set up for individual vendors inside the store. Each booth had a number and different types of antiques in the stall. A few held furniture, some glassware, one was all vintage books. The one closest to the front held vintage Christmas ornaments and an old aluminum tree from the 1950's.

Someone had made an effort to make the store smell nice. The scent of cinnamon and pine potpourri drifted to me. It should have been festive and cheery, but it didn't help at all with the eerie atmosphere of the shop.

As Leroy gathered images and information with his camera, my stomach was heavy and the skin across my back prickled. It was a sure sign that something wasn't right. I moved my hands to my pockets, feeling the bottles of potions and holy water zipped inside my jacket. That involuntary reflex had me frowning. I was no novice, but I hadn't felt quite this jumpy in a long time.

I eased forward, now keeping Leroy within arm's reach. While he was scrappy and tough, he still carried the scars from a lycanthropy case some twenty-five years prior. Not from an actual werewolf, but a serial killer who thought that he was one. Clinical lycanthropy was rare, but the attacker's delusions had still landed Leroy in the hospital. I vividly remembered going to visit him in Intensive Care when I was a little girl.

It had been one of my father's first paranormal cases, and it had left an impression on me. Even though the rational part of me knew that Leroy was competent and could protect himself if need be...I wouldn't take any chances with his safety. I dropped my eyes to his waist and noticed a modified holster at his belt. *He was carrying his taser tonight.*

That made me feel slightly better, because there was something very wrong inside the antique store. I could *feel* it, and seeing Leroy holding himself so stiffly as he filmed the room confirmed that he had felt it as well.

"We have a hit, in the far-right corner." Leroy's voice was a bare whisper. I watched as he panned back with the handheld device and tapped on a few buttons to 'store' an image.

Leaning over his shoulder, I checked the

screen for myself. While the majority of the room read in shades of yellow, the far-right corner was registering in much cooler colors. Green, blue, and finally purples radiated out from one dark shape.

The darker the color the colder the area was registering—which often meant a ghost or other paranormal activity.

"I'll check it out," I said, and moved forward quietly.

"Be careful," he said, and stayed well behind me and out of the way.

The fact that he did move back let me know that he was concerned. We'd definitely hit on something.

I moved directly to the far-right corner. My eyes passed over the booth filled with antiques. In the center of the booth on a wooden shelf I spotted a big, decorative metal urn.

"The urn," I breathed.

Leroy passed the thermal imaging camera over the area again. "Bingo."

I eased forward and held my hands barely above the surface of the urn's sides. It was ice cold. Carefully, I picked it up and checked underneath. In the low light I could barely make out the logo from a local funeral home. I blew out a relieved breath. At least now I knew what was causing the problem.

"Is that what I think it is?" Leroy's voice was low.

"It looks like a cremation urn," I said, setting it down. "Which would explain the haunting." I set the urn on a table. *For the love of god,* I thought. *My evening with Zakary had been ruined for this? A part-time paranormal investigator could have handled it.* I blew out an aggravated sigh. "The employees have probably been seeing a projection of whoever was interred."

"Some vendor put the urn on display in their booth, not even realizing what it actually was," Leroy said.

"It's probably the remains of a sweet old lady who had too many cats." Annoyed, I reached for the lid to check the contents.

"It still feels off." Leroy's voice was cautious. "I don't like it."

I gave the lid a quick twist and the seal broke with a muffled pop. Instantaneously the atmospheric pressure dropped, and the energy displacement hit me square in the chest.

"Oh, shit," I managed, right before all hell broke loose.

***

It was well after 2 o'clock in the morning by the time I arrived home. I waved tiredly at Leroy as he drove away with his headlights off. He wouldn't flip them back on until he was further down the road. I checked over my shoulder to make sure the neighbor wasn't spying out her window, and satisfied that the coast was clear, I walked across my yard in my stockinged feet. I crept up the deck steps, and set the black trash bag I'd been carrying in a big empty ceramic pot at the far corner of the deck.

The bag currently held my boots, and I did *not* want to bring them inside the house after what I'd recently walked through. Leroy kept heavy outdoor trash bags in his car for these situations, and I would deal with cleaning up my work boots in the morning. I drew a protection sigil in the air above the pot, then stopped to pull off my damp socks before I went inside. I had barely straightened when I heard the house phone ringing.

I still had a landline. It came in handy with my line of work, as it allowed for more privacy than a cell phone conversation. If it was ringing it meant one of two things: Family was calling, or somewhere—there was a serious paranormal problem.

Quickly, I let myself inside. Marching straight to the kitchen counter, I checked the caller ID. It was my father.

I picked up the receiver, but before I could speak, his voice came loud and clear over the phone. "What in the sweet hell is going on out there?"

I sighed. "Hello, Dad. How lovely to hear from you." The kitchen door shut gently behind me on its own. The light above the kitchen sink came on, washing the area with light.

"Don't you get snippy with me, young lady!" he snapped. "I was woken up by the most horrible dream. Are you all right? Is Leroy safe?"

"Yes," I said. "I am fine *and* Leroy is safe."

"Mandy, what in the hell are you up to?"

"Just doing my job."

He blew out an aggravated breath. "Listen, you know I wouldn't call at two in the morning unless I was worried. What happened tonight?"

I began emptying my pockets. "An investigation that should have been routine, ended up going six ways to hell."

"I hope you don't mean that literally." Dad's dry voice had me grinning despite myself.

"A local antique shop was complaining of paranormal activity, so we went out to investigate." I stopped from lining up the vials I'd carried on the counter and glanced down at my clothes. I was filthy. Ectoplasm and ash still clung to my jacket. Mud from the graveyard— my last stop for the evening—had splashed up to my knees. "It got a little messier than we bargained for."

"It was a silver colored urn. That was the problem, wasn't it?" Dad asked.

"Yes. It was. As usual your precognitive dreams are right on the money."

"I don't know if this classifies as precognition," Dad said. "More like a remote viewing, via dreams. I saw you opening an urn, and then the blowback."

I punched the button for the speaker and put the phone back in its cradle. "I need to peel out of the leather. Keep talking while I change."

"Okay," he said. "Do you still have that leather cleaner I got you?"

I walked over to the laundry room off the kitchen, pitching my voice so he could hear me. "Yes, I do."

"Was it a poltergeist or a level three entity at the antique store?" he asked.

"It was one pissed off spirit," I said, unzipping my jacket. "As soon as I broke the seal on the urn, she was released, and getting her contained made one hell of a mess."

"Did you dispose of the urn in the usual place?" he asked.

"At the old cemetery behind Notch Cliff," I said. Taking off the jacket, I hung it on special hooks on the laundry room wall. Once I shimmied out of the pants, I hung them beside the jacket to be dealt with in the morning.

"You disposed of it *inside* the gates, right?" My father stressed the word.

"Of course. Exactly as you taught me." I pulled two sticks of incense down from the cabinet above the washer and dryer and lit them. The aroma of sandalwood and dragon's blood stung the air.

"Good."

I waved the sticks back and forth, allowing their pungent smoke to float in front of me. "Her spirit should be at peace now that she's properly interred." I stepped in the fragrant smoke and fanned it around me.

"Are you wearing the Fifth Mars Pentacle talisman?" he asked.

I wasn't. I'd given the pendant to Estella. The silver talisman protected its wearer from possession and evil spirits. At the time I'd felt she'd had more urgent need of it. I slid my eyes guiltily toward the phone, and instead of out-and-out lying to my father, made a non-committal sound in reply.

"I sure hope you're doing a thorough cleansing," Dad's voice sounded from across the kitchen.

"I'm smudging, even as we speak," I said, and waved more smoke over the leather jacket and pants. I tucked the sticks into a ceramic holder and placed it on top of the washing machine. Which would allow the incense smoke to fill the laundry room area, and to start the cleansing process.

"Go take a shower and call me in the morning," Dad suggested.

Wearing only my camisole and underwear, I walked across to the kitchen phone. "I'll do that."

"Don't forget to scrub with sea salt!" Dad said, before I could disconnect the call.

My finger hovered above the button on the phone. "Dad, I am perfectly capable of taking care of myself."

"I know...it's just that sometimes, I worry."

I rolled my eyes. "Well stop worrying. Go enjoy your retirement and I'll text you in the morning."

"Get some sleep," he ordered.

"You do the same."

***

It took me hours to wind down and I didn't

fall asleep until almost five in the morning. When my alarm went off at seven, I almost wished I *would* have stayed up all night instead. Two miserable hours of sleep seemed worse than no sleep at all.

I shrugged on a robe, staggered down to the kitchen with the intention of starting a very large pot of coffee, and then the laborious process of cleaning my jacket and pants. But when I stepped into the kitchen doorway, I froze. The potion bottles I'd lined up on the counter last night were all knocked over, and the plastic container of holy water was in a puddle on the floor.

"What in the world?" I began, and Nyx strutted out from under the kitchen table. She sat herself next to the puddle of water and meowed, loudly.

"What's wrong, kitty?" I asked.

In answer, Nyx swatted at the bottle and it went on a lazy spin. I approached the spill carefully and saw for the first time the faintest outline of muddy footprints across the kitchen floor. They trailed over to the laundry room and then faded away.

"Damn it," I swore. I'd been so tired and distracted from my father's call last night that I'd unknowingly tracked graveyard dirt and cremation ash through my own kitchen.

"Meow." Nyx sounded smug.

"Aren't you clever?" I said to the cat. "Doing your best to clean up my mess?"

Nyx simply flipped her tail and began to clean her paws.

The coffee would have to wait. I went to the laundry room, pulled out the mop and a bucket. I began chanting a cleansing spell as I prepared to do a thorough scrub of my floor and an energetic cleansing of my kitchen. My Monday was off to a roaring start.

I made it to work on time, and the day drug on forever. I realized somewhere around lunch that I had a walloping case of the blues. Brought on, no doubt, by my exposure to the negative spirit, my fatigue from the banishing the night before, and the clean up work I'd had to do at home this morning.

I forced myself to speak politely to my co-workers and thought it best to limit my contact to the library patrons by staying put in my office for most of the day. I used the un-original excuse of catching up on paperwork. I managed to get a fair amount of work done, but my father had bombarded me with concerned text messages all day. Out of patience, I'd finally switched my cell phone to silent before I said— or texted—something I'd regret later. Nevertheless, by the end of my shift my mood had turned nasty.

The cheerful voices of the monthly book group as they gathered late in the afternoon sounded like nails on a chalkboard, and I found myself cringing away from their chatter. Instead of lingering to sit in on the discussion as usual, I slipped out the back and drove directly home.

It felt like every nerve I had was scraped raw.

I pulled in the driveway and cut the engine, and the simple act of climbing from my car had me gritting my teeth. Every joint and muscle ached. I'd only started up the steps of the deck when I spotted the trash bag filled with my boots from the night before.

"God damn it!" I swore. I'd forgotten to clean the boots, and even considering taking on that task had me struggling not to burst into tears.

Why did I even bother? I wondered. *It wasn't as if anyone in the village knew how much my family had sacrificed over the years...nor were they aware of the sheer number of times a Beaumont had risked life and limb protecting them from the multitude of paranormal threats in the area... No one cared, and even if they did know, they'd* never *accept all of this...Zakary, as wonderful as he was, would never understand my duty...*

My breath hitched in my chest and tears started to roll down my cheeks. "What does it even matter?" Hearing the pitifulness in my own voice had me jolting. Hard.

Fatigue and irritability were one thing, but bursting into tears and feeling depressed and hopeless was quite another. I was experiencing a serious depletion of my personal energy, meaning I had totally underestimated my exposure to that angry spirit.

This wasn't good. Not at all.

CHAPTER FOUR

Torn between anger and the beginnings of fear, I started up the deck steps. My heart pounded and my feet felt heavier than usual, causing me to stumble. Gripping the stair banister for support, I swore as everything around me went on a slow tilt. I had recognized far too late that whatever I'd tangled with last night had drained me to the point of exhaustion.

"No one to blame but yourself, Amanda," I muttered as I carefully made my way across the back deck. *Should have done a full banishing and protection ritual last night,* I thought. *But I hadn't.* Nor had I scrubbed with salt as my father had suggested. Instead I did a quick smudging, took a shower, and had tried to sleep.

Staggering toward the back door, I realized that I was going to have to swallow my pride, call my father, and have him work some healing and protection for me—long distance.

But first, I had to get inside.

I was reaching for the kitchen door when I heard my name being called. I turned too quickly and wobbled.

"Amanda!" Estella Flores Midnight was running full out. Her long dark hair was streaming behind her as she raced across the yard. And she wasn't alone.

"Estella?" *What was she doing here? Why was her sister Gabriella with her?* I frowned in confusion. "Did something happen at the Marquette mansion? Is the ghost of Victoria Midnight causing problems again?" My voice sounded slurred to my own ears.

Estella and Gabriella pounded up the steps, both running toward me. I saw their lips moving, knew they were speaking, but a loud buzzing noise drowned out their words.

"Amanda. Hey, Amanda!" Estella grabbed my arm.

"I'm sorry," I managed to say. "I'm not

feeling well."

"Are you sick?" Estella asked.

I shook my head hoping to clear it. "No, not sick. Drained."

"Were you hunting last night?" she whispered, slipping an arm around my waist.

I nodded and did my level best to stay on my feet.

"Were you injured?" Estella asked.

"Not physically," I said through gritted teeth. "But I seriously underestimated the damage to my astral body."

"Like psychic wounds?" Gabriella asked, reaching for my other arm.

"Damn it, you *are* hurt." Estella scowled. "Why didn't you call me, Amanda?"

"Because I thought I had time to take care of it myself." No sooner had I spoken, when my knees buckled.

"Estella," Gabriella said to her sister, "argue with her later. We need to get her inside and patch her up as quickly as possible."

The next thing I knew, I found myself sitting in the big comfy chair in my living room. It made me frown as I tried to puzzle it out. I didn't even remember walking inside the house...Not at all.

I blinked, and Estella and her sister were both up in my face. "Hi," I said.

"There you are," Estella said, and blew out a long relieved breath.

"Drink this." Gabriella pushed a mug into my hands.

I recognized the scent of tea. "Thank you," I murmured, and took a sip. It was loaded with sugar, and I drank deeply.

"The sugar will help snap you back from the psychic distress." Gabriella took a seat on the sofa across from me. "I also doctored it up using the herbs in your kitchen," she said.

"Thank you," I said again, realizing a bit too late that someone new was in the house. I swung my eyes around fully expecting that the house would throw a tantrum...But everything looked normal—as normal as it ever was, at any rate.

Gabriella was sitting on my sofa watching me, and there was Nyx climbing in her lap for some attention. The cat was purring loudly as the blonde gave her a face rub. It only took a glance at her to see that she'd figured out that I was a practitioner. The interior décor of my home wasn't exactly subtle.

Almost as if she knew what I'd been thinking, Gabriella smiled. "I love these moody blues you decorated with and the darker walls in your house. It's classy and witchy all at the same time. Like you are." She picked up a very old book on spell casting from the end table, scanned it and smiled. "I've been looking for this title for years." She flipped open the cover. "You've got a first edition too."

"It was a gift," I said, barely stopping myself before I added, *from my father.*

"How long have you been practicing?" Gabriella asked, conversationally.

I met her gaze squarely. "All my life." I leaned back in the chair and continued to drink my tea. Estella stood off to my right, her arms crossed over her chest, watching me. Her stance was protective and it was obvious that she was ready to spring into action if need be.

"What in the hell did you tangle with last night?" Estella wanted to know.

"More than I bargained for, apparently," I

answered her as honestly as I could.

"Don't you bullshit me!" Estella pointed one finger. "When I grabbed your arm to haul you in the house, you felt *bad*."

"Bad?" I frowned up at her.

"Yeah," she said. "The best way I can describe it was that I felt the need to go wash my hands immediately. Almost like you smelled bad."

Out of curiosity I lifted my arm and sniffed my own wrist.

"You don't actually stink," Estella assured me. "But I don't get why all of the sudden I don't want to stand too close to you."

"I felt it too," Gabriella said. "It made my stomach roil."

"Amanda, what in the hell is going on with you?" Estella asked.

I cleared my throat. "What you're describing, Estella, is your instinctual revulsion to the evil I'd combatted last night."

"Evil?" Gabriella's eyebrows went way up. "I think you'd better explain."

"Some people would have never noticed that anything was different about me today," I said.

"However, more sensitive individuals—such as witches or psychics—they would definitely notice something was off."

"And be repelled by it," Estella guessed.

"Precisely." I saluted her with the mug and drained it. Whatever witchery Gabriella had done to the tea was starting to work. I didn't feel nearly as shaky. "Thank you both for the help." I smiled at the two sisters. "I truly appreciate your kindness, but I should be able to take it from here."

"I'm not budging," Estella said. "I'm not leaving you alone until I know that you're going to be okay."

"Damn straight." Gabriella nodded in agreement. "You are still way too pale Amanda, and I can see that your aura is very muddy."

Estella considered her sister. "I thought only Cammy read auras."

Gabriella smiled. "I can see them too. And hers is full of shadows. Which means, we need to work a healing right away."

Resigned to the hard truth that they were right, I told myself to be grateful. *It could have been worse. Leroy could have been the one to*

find me passed out, or—gods help me—Zakary.
I yanked myself out of my musings in time to hear Gabriella say, "Do you have any healing crystals in the house, Amanda?"

"Yes." I nodded. "They're in the cabinet above the washer and dryer. There are also herbs, and several varieties of incense and plenty of different sorts of crystals."

"Her laundry room is right off the kitchen," Estella said, helpfully.

Gabriella set the cat aside and stood. "I'll go take a look, and pick out what we'll need."

"You will want to steer clear of the clothes hanging by the dryer," I warned her. "They may not be as *clean* as I thought they were, after all."

Gabriella merely nodded. "Okay. I'll go gather the supplies, and we can lay out a healing grid."

"A healing grid?" Estella cocked her head. "What's that?"

"A pattern of crystals and stones arranged around a person in such a way—" Gabriella cut herself off. "I'll show you in a minute."

I set the empty mug aside and stood, slowly.

"I need to get *all* of this psychic residue off me before we do that."

"How are you going to do that?" Estella wanted to know, as Gabriella headed for supplies.

"I'm going to start with a shower, and then a salt scrub." I took a step, wobbled and tried again.

Nyx pranced over to me, stopped suddenly, and hissed.

"Well, perfect," I said, as the cat ran away. "I guess she doesn't like the way I smell either."

"Come on, let me help you." Using her fingertips, Estella grabbed my elbow. "I'll stuff you in the shower and we'll get this party started."

"Thank you, Estella," I said, telling myself not to be embarrassed.

She gave my arm a squeeze. "What are friends for?"

After the shower and salt scrub, I was still wiped out, but felt less emotionally fragile. I wrapped my hair in a towel, and myself in my thick robe, and exited the master bathroom only to find Estella sitting on the foot of my bed, waiting for me.

"You look better, *prima*," she said.

"*Prima?*"

"Cousin," Estella translated, softly. "How do you feel now?"

"Stronger." I smiled. "I hope I smell better, anyway."

Estella bounced to her feet, leaned in, and gave a dramatic sniff. "You smell good to me. Is that my sandalwood and rose soap?"

"It is. I figured this would be the perfect time to try it out."

"Gabriella is waiting downstairs. She's got that healing grid thingy all laid out."

I pulled the towel down and rubbed it over my hair. "How much did you tell her?"

"About you being a secret member of the Midnight family?" Estella gave me a bland stare. "I didn't say anything."

The tension in my shoulders lessened. "Thank you."

"Considering the state you were in when we found you," Estella said, "and the little bit of information that you *did* tell her, Gabriella is going to wonder what the hell you've been up to."

I reached for a wide tooth comb on my dresser. "I'll tell her as much as I can." I reached up to work the comb through my hair, and my hands began to shake.

"Give me that." Estella snatched the comb away, pushed me to sit on the end of my bed, and started to work the tangles out herself. "*Aye dios mió!*" she grumbled, and continued to mutter under her breath in Spanish while she combed out my hair.

Despite myself, I started to smile.

Estella worked her way through the tangles and then she paused. "Wow," she said, pulling down the collar of my robe. "You've got tattoos all over your back."

I turned to regard her over my shoulder. "They are much more than that. They're actually protective sigils and runes."

"Can I see them?" Estella asked.

There was no point in being shy, I loosened my robe and shrugged free, letting the back drop down to my waist.

"They're beautiful," she said, pushing my hair out of the way. "I really dig the phases of the moon down your spine."

"Thank you."

"What's this one?" She touched a finger in the center of my right shoulder blade.

"It's a bind rune made of old Norse symbols."

"And this?" She touched the opposite shoulder.

"The Celtic triple knot, a triquetra."

"There's a classic pentagram, and more symbols I don't recognize. "This writing under this symbol over here..." She touched my lower back to indicate the spot. "Is that Hebrew?"

"Yes. It's a Pentacle from the Key of Solomon," I explained.

She touched another tattoo along my side. "What's this cool, ancient looking writing?"

"That's Enochian—also known as Angelic," I explained.

"I see some Egyptian symbols too. The eye of Horus, and an ankh...Damn, you covered pretty much all of your bases, didn't you?"

"That's the idea."

"Hey, how is she doing?" Gabriella's voice preceded her into the room.

I stiffened, as my naked back was facing the door.

"Wow," Gabriella said, obviously seeing the tattoos.

Belatedly, I shrugged the robe back in place. I could thank my fatigue for not being aware that Gabriella had been approaching. Resigned, I tied the belt and stood to face her.

"You're a Guardian, aren't you?" Gabriella's voice was almost reverent.

"Yes," I said.

Estella's eyebrows went way up as she looked from me to her sister. "You know about Guardians?"

Gabriella nodded. "Grandpa told me about them when I was fifteen years old."

Estella blinked. "He did?"

"As a son of Midnight," I said quietly, "it would have been his duty to pass along that information to one member of the next generation."

Gabriella nodded. "I was the one."

"Wait," Estella broke in. "You mean he didn't tell Dru or Cammy?"

Gabriella shook her head. "No. Drusilla was

already pulling away and trying to hide her abilities, and in regards to Cammy...my grandparents worried that she'd lack the discretion necessary to handle that particular information while she was a teen."

A small weight had been lifted off my shoulders, but I was still cautious. "May I ask what he told you, Gabriella?"

"That if there was ever a magickal or paranormal foe beyond our capabilities, that I should speak to Leroy Holtgrave. That he would know who to put me in contact with," she said. "Grandpa stressed never to contact the Guardian lightly."

I hugged my elbows, feeling chilled. "I see."

Gabriella narrowed her eyes. "He made it sound as if they were all men—at least that's what I assumed."

"Until me, they all were," I admitted. "I was the first female born in the Beaumont family for several generations."

Gabriella grinned. "Ha! A tradition breaker. Just like my daughter, Danielle."

Estella shrugged. "It's weird that Gabriella happened to be the one who was with me today."

"More like fate." Gabriella shrugged. "Things have a way of working out as they are intended. I learned that for myself a long time ago."

"I trust that you will keep this information private," I said, studying Gabriella. Despite their very different coloring, she and Estella strongly resembled each other. Same wavy hair, similarly shaped face and mouth.

"Of course, I'll keep your confidence." Gabriella nodded. "I promised my grandfather I wouldn't ever tell Dru or Cammy, and I haven't."

"Thank you," I said.

"Let's get this healing work started." Gabriella's voice was brisk. "You're swaying on your feet."

"Let me get dressed," I said.

"I'll be downstairs." Gabriella eased out of the doorway and headed back down.

I managed to dress myself and slipped into a pair of flannel pajama pants and a comfy sweatshirt. As soon as I'd finished, Estella looped an arm around my waist.

"Come on," she said. "I want to see how this healing grid works, anyway."

"This will be a very practical magickal lesson for you," I said wryly, and tried not to lean on her too heavily as we started to the stairs.

Estella gave my waist a squeeze. "I'm only interested in seeing that you get better."

***

I felt more like myself after Gabriella completed her work. Once we were finished, she went home to her husband and daughter. Estella had insisted on staying and even took on the job of cleansing my boots, jacket and pants. I was worried it might be too much for her to handle, but she listened carefully to my instructions and went about the task competently, with no fuss.

I woke up from a nap a few hours later and followed my nose to the kitchen. Estella had made herself at home and was preparing some soup. She was standing at the stove making grilled cheese, and there was a thick book in a stand on the counter at her elbow. I saw that she was reading over one of my father's books on spirit possession and hauntings.

"Hi," I said.

"Hey!" she smiled. "You look better."

I yawned. "I feel more like myself."

"Are you hungry?" she asked. "I did the standard can of chicken soup and grilled cheese."

"That sounds perfect."

"Go sit and I'll get this dished up."

I sat at the table, and Nyx jumped on an empty chair to join me. I passed my hand over the head of the cat and was relieved when she allowed me to pet her.

Estella served the soup and sandwiches and shooed Nyx out of the chair to sit beside me. I started to dig in, knowing that the food would help me to recover as much as the healing magick.

"Your father called while you were napping."

"Oh?" I said. "Should I start apologizing now?" I hoped he had at least been civil.

Estella chuckled. "Once I got him to calm down and listen, instead of bombarding me with questions, he was fine."

"I see," I said taking a bite of grilled cheese. "I'd kill to know what spell you used to get him to stop talking."

Estella grinned. "I liked Vic."

I swallowed quickly. "*Vic?*"

"Victor Eugene Beaumont the Fourth, is a hell of a mouthful. He said I could call him Vic. Besides, he and your mom were pretty worried about you."

My father would never allow me to live this down, I thought. "I'll text them both later this evening."

"Zak called as well." Estella said. "I told the deputy that you had a bug and were resting." Before I could comment she continued. "I think Zak would have come over himself, but I talked him out of it."

"I appreciate that." I said and meant it. "I'm beyond grateful for your help today—yours and Gabriella's."

"After supper I'll load up the dishwasher for you and head home so you can get some sleep. No offense, but you look rough. There's still some big-ass circles under your eyes."

"Nothing a good night's sleep won't cure." I hoped.

Estella was good to her word, and after supper I got myself a huge glass of water, headed upstairs and climbed straight under the covers. Nyx jumped up and made herself at home on the foot of the bed. I exchanged a few text messages with my parents and set the phone on the nightstand charger.

I'd only started to doze off when my cell rang. It was Zakary.

I picked it up and hit accept. "Hello?"

"How are you doing?" His voice was filled with genuine concern. "Estella told me you have the flu."

"I'll be good as new in a few days," I assured him.

"Do you need anything? I could run to the store bring you whatever you need. Cold medicine, tissues..."

"I'm fine," I assured him, touched at his generosity. "All set. But thank you anyway."

"Okay. Why don't I give you a call tomorrow and check on you?"

Despite myself, I smiled. "That would be

nice."

"Get some rest," he said. "I'll talk to you in the morning."

"Good night, Zakary."

"Good night, Amanda."

I ended the call and replaced the phone on the charger. With a sigh I rolled over and fell asleep instantly.

The next morning I called in sick, going with the uninspired excuse of having the flu. It wasn't too much of a stretch either, because that's exactly how I felt. I soaked in the tub after breakfast using essential oils and more sea salt. I scrubbed myself down again with the sandalwood- rose soap Estella had given me, and after I dressed for the day, I worked the Lesser Banishing Ritual of the Pentagram.

I should have done that right after the case the other night, but there was no point in indulging in hindsight. Once the ritual was finished I took the rest of the morning and reinforced the wards on my home and surrounding property. Clearly, I'd gotten too lax, and I didn't want to ever go through this sort of situation again...not if I could help it.

Leroy called and checked on me as well. He was far too clever to buy 'the flu' cover story, and I ended up getting a firm scolding for not being more diligent with working personal protection and cleansing magicks after an investigation.

He filled me in on his findings on the serial number and funeral home mark on the urn. He had also identified the remains. "Yeah," he said. "Brace yourself, but that wasn't a sweet old lady you let loose."

I listened in shocked surprise as he spoke. The remains belonged to a woman who'd been accused of murdering her husband. She'd passed away before the case had ever been brought to trial, back in the 1980's. According to Leroy's research, the evidence had been overwhelming and consequently, her family had shunned her.

"The angry spirit of a murderer, who's remains had been abandoned." I shook my head over the news. No wonder I'd been knocked for a loop.

"Well, Toots, it's a good reminder to *never* take an investigation casually again," Leroy said.

"Yes, you are absolutely right."

"Get some rest." His voice was brusque. "I'll call tonight and check on you again."

I'd no sooner disconnected the call when there was a brisk rap on the front door. I rarely used that entrance. Curious, I went to the door, opened it, and found a floral delivery person on my tiny stone stoop.

"Delivery for Amanda Beaumont," he said, passing me a huge arrangement wrapped in protective paper.

"Thank you," I said, surprised.

I shut the door and carried the vase of flowers into the living room. I placed them on the coffee table and carefully ripped the paper away to reveal blossoms that were bright and in warm autumn colors. There were yellow carnations, sunflowers, golden yarrow, orange roses and bronze chrysanthemums in the arrangement. I pulled the envelope holding the enclosure card and read the message.

Get well soon, gorgeous was scrawled across the card. "Oh Zakary." I smiled, and indulged myself with some sniffing and sighing over the blossoms.

Nyx rested her paws on the table and sniffed at the flowers too.

"I'm in real trouble, Nyx," I said to the cat.

"*Meow*?" Nyx pawed at the vase.

"Zakary Parker is far too kind, sweet and caring. I could fall for him easily, and all I've done since the moment we met, is lie to him."

I would need to think carefully about this, and how best to proceed. I patted the head of a spicy carnation, and wondered how much the sexy deputy would be able to handle. I knew one thing for sure: I couldn't keep pretending to be someone I wasn't.

Not with him. Quite frankly Zakary deserved better. Perhaps he would be able to understand my responsibility to the community, and even accept my heritage.

If he was unable to...then I would have to walk away.

No matter how much it hurt.

CHAPTER FIVE

Tuesday morning I got up, put on a pair of comfortable jeans, thick socks, and layered a plaid flannel shirt over a cami. I had decided the night before to give myself another day off to fully recuperate.

I puttered around the house, and after using the leather cleaner for a second time to ritually cleanse the outfit I wore on investigations, I decided to work even more magickal protection into the jacket.

I pulled out my sewing basket, selected deep purple embroidery floss and, using a satin stitch, I began to embroider warding runes all around the inner cuffs of my jacket.

I spent a quiet and cozy morning sipping at a giant mug of tea and adding the symbols to the inside of the stretchy cuffs. Here, they wouldn't be seen, but they'd be in a location that I would be able to *feel* them against my skin. I chanted while I embroidered, weaving more power into the sigils, and by the time I finished there were nine runes in a circle around the interior of each jacket cuff.

I snipped the final thread and stood. Slipping the jacket on, I gave my arms an experimental shake. The magick of the runes began to activate immediately, and I felt a tingle run up both arms and across my shoulders. I crossed my wrists in front of my chest so that both cuffs were pressed together.

Taking a deep breath, I formally sealed the spell. "By all the power of three times three; link these runes together for safety. A shield to defend me from spirits and foe; round and round this protection magick will flow..."

I focused, holding the cuffs up to eye level and added a bit of my own personal power to ensure that the runes and their energies were bound to the garment permanently. Finally, I closed up the spell in the way my father had taught me.

After lowering my arms, I wasn't surprised to discover that the cuffs of the jacket felt heavier now—almost as if there were metal bracelets inside of the cuffs instead of the silken thread I'd sewn on. Pleased with the results, I hung the jacket back on a wooden hanger and tucked it neatly in my closet.

I had just finished tidying up when I received a few more visitors. Gabriella Midnight-Marquette and her baby, Danielle. "Hey!" Gabriella greeted me with a big smile. "We wanted to stop by and bring you lunch."

I was momentarily caught off-guard at the kind gesture, but recovered quickly, and invited them inside. "Welcome friends," I said formally, before Gabriella crossed the kitchen threshold. On cue, the overhead light in the kitchen became brighter.

Gabriella had her daughter on one hip, and a diaper bag and canvas grocery bag slung over her opposite shoulder. "You look better!" she said. The door shut behind her on its own, and Gabriella either didn't notice, or she chose not to react.

"Thank you. I am feeling much better." I

smiled at the baby in her coat and knit aqua blue hat. "And this must be Danielle."

Danielle squealed out a response. I held out my hands to the baby and she reached for me. While Gabriella removed her own coat, I unzipped the baby's. A short time later we were all seated at the table.

"Can't go wrong with a good vegetable soup," Gabriella said, pulling to-go containers out of the bag. "Like my Gran always says: *this is sure to fix what ails you.*"

I bounced the baby on my knee and slid the flowers from Zakary farther out of her reach. "That sounds wonderful. What about the baby, won't she be hungry?"

"I fed her before we came over," Gabriella said. "She'll be happy enough with a cracker or two. By the way, nice flowers."

"Thanks."

"That's quite the floral message." Gabriella raised her eyebrows. "Carnations for energy and yarrow for magickal protection and healing. Sunflowers for adoration, and you've been given orange roses too. Those symbolize fascination and desire, not to mention the chrysanthemums—"

"Which ward off ghosts." I finished for her.

Gabriella took her seat. "Who's the sender?"

"The flowers are from Zakary Parker," I said, trying to act casual.

"Mama," Danielle said, reaching for her mother.

"Deputy Parker?" Gabriella asked as she took her daughter back. "Well, well...the man has excellent taste in flowers. I knew I liked him."

After we'd eaten, we moved to the living room where eight-month-old Danielle decided to entertain us by showing off her new cruising skills. The cat stayed just out of reach, and the baby was very determined to get to the cat. Around the coffee table they went, while Gabriella and I chatted.

Gabriella braced her foot against the table, allowing the baby to lean on her outstretched leg and regain her balance. "I'll be honest," she began, "I had another reason for dropping by today."

"Oh?" I glanced over at the blonde.

"There's a serious paranormal problem at the

mansion. It's starting to concern me," Gabriella said. "We thought after the lost dowry had been found and returned to the Ames family, things would settle down."

"And they haven't?"

"For a time they did," Gabriella said. "Then Estella came to town and everything changed —"

Gabriella broke off when Danielle plopped down to her butt and looked around in surprise.

"How did it change, exactly?" I asked.

Gabriella helped Danielle gain her feet again. "Estella told me that she confided in you about her and Chauncey's experiences at the mansion, and their interaction with the ghost of Pierre-Michel."

I nodded as the baby smacked her hands against the coffee table and began to babble in earnest to the cat. "Yes, she has." I pitched my voice over Danielle.

Gabriella fished in the diaper bag, produced a teething ring and handed it to the baby. Danielle dropped back to her butt and began to gnaw on it with gusto. "Ever since the night of the Grand Opening in October," she said, "the ghosts have ramped up the activity."

"The night that Victoria and Pierre-Michel possessed Estella and Chauncey."

"Correct." Gabriella leaned back against the couch. "I've consulted with Cammy, but she has done all she can. Her background is in research and documentation, not—"

"Removal," I finished for her.

"Exactly," Gabriella said. "Several times in the past month I've woken up to hear talking in the baby's room. We do have a video monitor in the nursery, and while we've *seen* nothing, Cammy did manage to get an EVP of a child's voice."

I felt a chill roll down my back at the thought of interactive spirits in the baby's room. When I spoke, I made sure my voice would be calm. "Did you happen to catch any words?"

"It was in French," Gabriella said.

"What did the spirit say?"

"Philippe wouldn't tell me." Gabriella passed her hand over her daughter's dark hair.

"How much do you know about the history of the home. Do you know if any children passed away there?"

"We've been digging into his family tree hard in the past few weeks," she admitted. "Philippe's grandfather Henri pulled an old family bible from the family's estate in France, and we discovered that Claude and Pierre-Michel *did* have other siblings. A brother that died when he was only four years old."

"He died while living at the mansion?" I wanted to clarify.

"It seems that was the case. It's odd as he wasn't listed on the formal family tree. There was simply a handwritten entry of his birth and death in a bible that had belonged to Pierre-Michel and Claude's mother. So we were *very* surprised to learn about him."

I pulled my cell from my pocket. "What was his name, date of birth and so forth?"

"Jacques." She shuddered. "He was born in 1824 and died in 1828."

"Have you had any interactions with the ghost of a child before now?" I asked, making a note in my phone.

"Last Thanksgiving Jaime Ames and Cammy both saw the ghost of a little boy."

"The one that she followed to the western

wing and found the dowry," I said, remembering the story Cammy had shared at the ghost tour.

"Right." Gabriella nodded. "We all thought that what they saw was a sort of memory—an *etheric imprint*, Cammy called it."

"Which led you to assume that her vision of the three boys playing in the nursery was simply something happy that the house had held on to."

"It was what we thought at the time. Now I'm not so sure."

"What you are describing, Gabriella, is a residual style haunt and not uncommon."

"For the past year we'd all assumed that the boy she'd followed was a vision or projection, I suppose, of one of Claude and Amelia's sons. Three of their five sons lived in the house in Illinois for the first years of their lives."

"Now you're wondering if the voice in Danielle's nursery is that of the boy who died so long ago?"

"Yes, I do. Because all of Claude and Amelia's sons survived to adulthood. But with Jacques Marquette, why did no one record his birth on the family register?" Gabriella said. "Why was it hidden?"

I nodded. "I'll dig into the local archives, cemetery records, and check the birth announcements and obituaries for 1824 and 1828, to see what I can find."

Gabriella fidgeted. "I wanted to, but was afraid of what I would find."

"Were you aware that forty percent of children born during that time period never lived past the age of five? It's a sad fact, but it was common. There is no reason to be afraid of research."

"I wasn't spooked until after Philippe listened to the EVP recording that Cammy captured. I could tell that it alarmed him because he's had Danielle sleeping in our room with us, ever since."

I'd have to speak to her husband and find out exactly what the voice had said, I thought to myself. "He is concerned about this as well?" I asked as politely as possible.

"First the possession happened to Estella and Chauncey, and next the voice in the nursery...that's when Philippe asked me if there was anyone who could help us *remove* the ghosts." Gabriella held my gaze. "That was when I thought to call you. Philippe doesn't know about the Guardians. All he knows is that I am going to speak to an expert."

"I appreciate your discretion..." I began, but was distracted by the baby pulling herself back up, using the leg of my jeans for support.

"Can you help us?" Gabriella asked.

Before I could answer, Danielle held up her arms wanting to be picked up. I complied, and when the baby smiled at me, my heart fell completely. Perhaps it was because we were distantly related. I wasn't sure, but I cuddled the baby on my lap anyway. She was so small and innocent... "Of course," I said, making up my mind on the spot. "I will do whatever I can to help you and your family."

Gabriella sighed in relief. "Thank you. None of us have been sleeping very well."

"I will contact a colleague of mine and we'll get to work right away. Are there any events at the mansion this weekend?"

"A small wedding reception on Friday night, that brought a few bookings to the suites for

Friday and Saturday night."

"How about Sunday night?" I asked. "Are you clear?"

"Yes we are." Gabriella shook her head. "There's nothing booked for Sunday."

"Perfect," I said. "I'll want access to the office space on the first floor, the museum room, and the public side of the mansion. I need for the family wing to be completely clear as well."

"You can have full access."

Danielle wanted down, so I allowed her to slide to the floor. She immediately began cruising along the coffee table again. "It would be best if you, Philippe, and the baby vacated the house for the night," I said. "Perhaps you can stay with your grandmother."

"We could."

"What about your brother-in-law?" I asked.

"Chauncey has been living in the detached carriage house out back. It's two stories, with a garage on the lower level and a couple rooms above."

I tried to recall if I'd ever seen it. "When did he move into the carriage house?"

"About a month ago," Gabriella said.

Right after he'd been possessed by the spirit of his ancestor, I realized.

Gabriella continued. "We'd been using the old carriage house as a garage for our cars and for storage. But Chauncey decided he'd like to have an apartment there, where he could be close by, but still have his own place."

"Sure," I said. "I can see that."

Gabriella grinned. "The kitchenette and bathroom plumbing were a hot mess, and once he got that sorted out, it was mostly cosmetic. As soon as it was livable, he was determined to move right in."

Because he wanted his own space, or because he needed to get away from the haunting? I wondered. Out loud I said, "We'll need him in the loop, so he won't disturb us while we're working."

Gabriella nodded. "No problem. I'll give him a heads up."

"I'll contact my associate and we'll shoot for Sunday night."

"Perfect." Gabriella scooped up Danielle, who'd begun to fuss. "Somebody could use a nap." She stood and picked up the diaper bag.

"I'll see what I can do about making it so you can all rest easier," I promised, picking up the toy and holding it out to the baby. "In the meantime there are a few amulets and seals you can put in the baby's room and in yours that should repel any spirits from wandering in."

Danielle took her toy and dropped her head against her mother's shoulder.

Gabriella patted her daughter's back. "Thank you, Amanda. I'll take whatever I can get."

"Let me gather a few things for you to take home." I rested my hand gently on the baby's back. "I promise, Gabriella. Whatever I can do to help your family, I will."

***

Leroy was thrilled with the opportunity to take all of his gizmos up to the mansion. The only wrinkle in my plan came when Estella asked if she could join us. I had a list of very salient reasons why she shouldn't—but as she pointed out—she was one of the people the ghosts had been picking on.

Estella promised me that she would hit the books and study before Sunday, as well as do whatever she was told during the investigation. I knew she wasn't keen on being up at the mansion, and the fact that she was eager to go and confront the very thing that made her uncomfortable spoke volumes.

I discussed the situation with Leroy, and he seemed to think having her there might entice the spirits to put in appearance. "After all," he said, "we can't remove those suckers if we can't find them."

I spent the rest of the week researching and preparing for Sunday night. Zakary dropped by my office on Thursday, surprising me with soup and sandwiches. We sat in my office, on either side of my desk, chatting and eating our lunch. I tried to broach the topic of the paranormal with him in an attempt to see how he would react to my heritage, but before we got very far we were interrupted.

Jenna Ames, one of the part-time staff, stuck her head in my door. "Amanda, excuse me. But I thought you'd want to know that Philippe Marquette is here for your one o'clock meeting."

"I should have called first," Zakary said. "I'll head out and leave you to your meeting."

"Thank you for lunch," I managed to say before he dropped a quick kiss on my mouth. The kiss had totally caught me off guard. He'd never kissed me in public before. Zakary left with a cheerful wave so I could take my meeting.

I ignored Jenna's grin and shut the door to my office so Philippe Marquette and I would have the opportunity speak privately. Philippe wasted no time and shared the translation of the EVP Cammy had captured. *'I'm scared,'* the young voice had said. I sat behind my desk and listened carefully to the recording several times. It was definitely a child, and while he'd had to translate for me, the tone of the voice was troubling.

"I did some research in the past few days," I said to Philippe. "There is a record of Jacques Marquette's death. I also found where he was buried."

Philippe leaned back in his chair. "You did? How?"

"Through the records of burials at the local cemeteries. There's an old cemetery behind Notch Cliff. He's interred there." I slipped my phone out of my top drawer, opened my photo app, and showed him the picture of a worn stone monument with a lamb resting on the top. The headstone was engraved simply with the name *Jacques L. Marquette* and the dates of his birth and the too soon date of his death.

"I wasn't aware there was a cemetery behind the cliffs."

"It's forgotten mostly," I said. "I realize it's not the same cemetery where Pierre-Michel and his mother are buried."

Philippe frowned. "That's odd, don't you think?"

I folded my hands on my desk. "Perhaps it was that his mother wanted him close to the mansion, somewhere she could walk to and visit the grave, everyday."

Philippe gave me a bland look. "Do *you* have any theories why his birth and death weren't listed on the family register?" he asked.

"I have a few," I said.

"Such as?"

I adjusted my glasses and met his gaze squarely. "Since the birth was only recorded in his mother's bible—but not the official family register—I would surmise that either it was too painful to discuss, or that he was *her* child, but possibly not her husband's."

Philippe didn't so much as blink. "The story goes that Emile—Claude and Pierre-Michel's father—was a hard and unkind man."

"It's only a theory." I shrugged. "Perhaps losing one of his sons at such a young age made him that way. We'll never know."

"I've always thought the house held many secrets," Philippe said, thoughtfully. "I wonder if we will ever know them all?" He stood. "Thank you for your time, Mademoiselle Beaumont, and for your help."

I nodded and showed the man out. Philippe Marquette was a devoted husband and father, yet his comment about secrets bothered me. I stood in my office, taking in the carefully cultivated cover I'd built for myself.

It was a part of me. God knows I'd worked brutally hard for my degrees. I enjoyed my work in the library, and being a part of the community. My role as head librarian was the public face that I allowed people to see. The rest had to remain private.

The less people that actually knew about the Guardians the better. *Sometimes*, I reminded myself, *secrets were vital*. Now and then, secrets were in place to protect others, not from the truth, but to shelter them from harm.

***

Leroy and I met up at the mansion Sunday night, right before sunset. I saw that Estella was already there. I spotted the old family truck she drove, parked in the winery parking lot.

I pulled my satchel out of the passenger seat and swung it over my shoulder. There was a thunderstorm moving in, but it wasn't forecast to hit until after midnight. "We got lucky with the weather," I called to Leroy as he closed the trunk of his car and gathered up his equipment bags.

"Nothing like a good electrical storm to boost the atmosphere," he agreed.

I tugged my jacket's zipper higher. The

temperatures were in the 40's but a stiff wind was pushing the storm front farther east. Tonight I'd dressed for comfort in a soft lace camisole, dark jeans and my sturdy, low heeled boots. My magickally enhanced leather jacket made me feel more confident, and as I walked forward surveying the house, I had a feeling I was going to need every trick at my disposal tonight.

"How are you feeling?" Leroy asked as we moved down the small brick walkway, hauling our bags full of various equipment.

"Excited and raring to go," I said, tucking a stray tendril of hair behind my ear. "Taking a few days off allowed me to recoup the lost energy. I've waited years to finally get to the bottom of the haunting in the mansion."

"Me too, Mandy." Leroy grinned at me. "Me too." He knocked on the private entrance and was greeted at the door by Philippe Marquette.

"Welcome. Gabriella is packing a few last things for the baby," he explained. "We'll be leaving shortly."

Leroy shook his hand. "I appreciate that tour of the house you gave me earlier this week,

Philippe. It will make tonight go much more smoothly."

Philippe stepped back and as I walked across the threshold of the house, the runes stitched inside the cuffs flared to life. I didn't react to the arcane warning, but instead smiled blandly and said hello.

"Did you turn off the heat like we discussed?" Leroy asked the Frenchman.

"Yes." Philippe nodded. "All the lights and computers are off as well."

"*Andale!*" Estella's voice carried down the stairs. "Let's move, Gabriella."

The sisters came down the stairs together. Estella was toting a large diaper bag and a cat carrier, while Gabriella was trying to hold on to a very ticked-off Danielle. The baby was squirming in her mother's arms and howling the walls down.

I was surprised to hear the baby making such a ruckus. She'd been so mellow and happy the last time I'd seen her.

"*Ma belle?*" Philippe looked concerned.

"She's a bit out of sorts," Gabriella said grimacing as the baby tried to climb out of her arms.

Estella set the cat carrier down carefully, placed the diaper bag by the front door, and held out her hands for her niece. "Come here, *mija*."

Danielle flung herself towards Estella.

"Good grief." Gabriella rolled her eyes to the ceiling. "I've never seen her throw such a hissy fit before."

Estella ran her hand over the baby's head, and Danielle began settle down. "Maybe she's over tired," Estella said as the baby clung to her. "I can carry her out to the car for you guys."

"Thank you, Estella." Philippe smiled.

Before Estella managed to take a single step toward the door, there was a loud thud from the floor above, and then the unmistakable sound of running feet and laughter.

CHAPTER SIX

"Is there anyone else in the house?" I asked.

"No, there is not," Philippe said.

I headed to the base of the staircase and listened intently, while Leroy scrambled for his recorders and cameras. As we all stood in the lobby waiting to see what would happen next, the laughter seemed to get louder...almost as if there were children playing. The ambient temperature suddenly dropped, and that sound of running feet began to travel down the stairs toward us.

Gabriella hustled away from the steps and Philippe pulled his wife close. Together the couple moved to stand protectively in front of Estella and the baby.

Leroy slapped his thermal camera on and

aimed it at the steps. I felt the displacement of energy as the spirit rushed past me and the door that led to the public side of the house was flung open. Gabriella flinched as the door slowly closed and the sound of a child's laughter drifted away.

"Well..." Gabriella's voice was strained. "*That* was new."

***

Once Philippe, Gabriella and their daughter left, we got down to business. Thanks to Leroy's tour earlier in the week, we had already gathered our baseline data, and we knew exactly where the 'hot spots' were.

Three main areas of activity had been confirmed. One was in the baby's room, the other in the western wing on the third floor by the window seat—the very spot where the ghosts of Pierre-Michel and Victoria Midnight had taken advantage of Chauncey and Estella, and last but not least, the museum room that held the portrait.

Estella came back down the staircase with a

flashlight. "Everything is off in the family wing. I double checked."

"Thanks, Toots," Leroy said, checking the monitors that he'd set up in the eastern lobby.

"Toots?" Estella sent him a hard look.

"Mandy," he said to me, completely oblivious, "will you go and adjust the camera in the museum room slightly to the left?"

I went down the hallway to make the correction, and left them to it. They needed to work out the pecking order for themselves.

"Listen old man..." Estella's voice carried clearly. "If you call me *Toots* one more time, I'll mop the floor with you."

I returned in time to see that Leroy had never even glanced up at her. "Your kind has a rule about harming none, don't they?"

Estella sputtered. "My *kind*?"

Leroy fine tuned the brightness on a second monitor. "Yeah, witches. You know 'harm none'."

"I'm not a *bruja*—witch. Not yet anyway," Estella said. "And even if I were, I'd be happy to make an exception in your case."

"Play nice, children," I told the pair of them,

and secured a loose pin in the bun at the nape of my neck.

Estella sent me an incredulous look. "He does realize that he can't go around calling women 'Toots', doesn't he?"

"You don't like nicknames?" Leroy scratched his chin. "How 'bout I call you, Dollface?"

"*Eres un idiota.*" Estella shook her head.

I was pretty sure she'd called him an idiot, and I bit down on my lip to keep from laughing out loud.

"What?" Leroy frowned at Estella. "I call my granddaughter Dollface all the time."

Before things could get more out of hand I changed the topic. "Are we monitoring the staircase from the family area into the eastern lobby?"

"We are now," Leroy said, pointing to another infrared camera. "I wish I would have caught that first manifestation on camera..."

"Nobody saw that coming." Estella reached up and touched the Fifth Mars Pentacle talisman I'd given her weeks ago. "Why does it seem creepier when it's the ghost of a child?" she wondered out loud.

Leroy focused on her. "If you don't think you are up to this—"

"I didn't say that." Estella scowled at him. "I've been possessed by one of the god damn ghosts that hangs out here. I have more of a reason to be here than you, *anciano*. I want this haunting over with, for me and for my family!"

I wondered if Estella realized that she'd referred to the Midnights as her family. I don't think I'd ever heard her call them that before. I decided not to comment, and instead held up a hand for peace. "Lets all stop arguing and get started."

Leroy shifted his attention back to his equipment. "Sounds good to me."

***

It seemed that the spirit of the child was done with his performance for the evening. It was all quiet in the family wing and remained so for the next few hours. The window seat area on the third floor had elevated readings, but again the ghosts were a no show.

As we neared the end of the evening, Leroy

decided to carefully scan the antiques and ephemera in the cases of the museum room himself. Not surprisingly, the portrait maintained the highest energetic readings. Estella had offered to go in the room alone to see if she could draw the spirit of Pierre-Michel out, but I swiftly vetoed that idea.

After his sweep with the handheld devices Leroy decided to stay in the eastern lobby and watch the monitors until dawn. Estella and I made a final sweep of the public areas of the house, on the off chance that something would put in an appearance. I watched her carefully as we toured the third floor of the western wing together, but she was fine. The talisman was obviously working for her.

"Why don't we walk through the ballroom again?" I suggested.

Estella nodded. "That's not a bad idea. I had a flashback to a memory of Victoria and Pierre-Michel dancing together there."

Together she and I descended the stairs and swung into the hallway. There was a flickering light coming from the room and it washed out into the darkened corridor.

"What is that?" Estella whispered, pointing at the flashing lights. "That shouldn't be happening. All of the lights were turned off."

As we moved closer I felt the temperature drop. "Paranormal activity," I said to her. "This is what we've been waiting for." I was about to walk in, but paused when I saw Leroy hustling down the hall from the opposite direction.

"I saw someone walk in the museum room and the readings went off the scale," he said quietly.

"Human or spirit?" I asked him.

"It happened so fast," Leroy said. "I'm not sure. The equipment went insane."

Estella touched the sleeve of my jacket to get my attention. "What's the play?"

"Remember what we talked about," I whispered. "Stay back. Wait out in the hall until I call for you, then *if* I do, you may come in."

She nodded. "Understood."

"If I call you to come in, promise to stay behind me no matter what you see or hear."

She nodded again, and I gave my full attention to the museum room. Together, Leroy and I began to cautiously approach the room.

We eased inside and I discovered a dark-haired man. He stood perfectly still, his back to us, staring up at the portrait on the wall—and he was corporeal.

My heartbeat sped up. The man shifted his head slightly, and I recognized him. It was Chauncey Marquette. My stomach tightened painfully as I took in his appearance. His hair was disheveled, and he was barefoot and only wearing a pair of pajama pants.

Leroy shifted to get a better view of the room. He gave me a look that was all raised eyebrows, but he remained silent.

"Mr. Marquette," I said calmly, "Chauncey, you're interrupting our investigation. Did you forget that we would be here tonight?"

He turned around and his eyes raked over me.

For a split second I was distracted by all the lean muscle that was on display, however the look in his eyes was all wrong. Chauncey muttered in French and I shot a quick side glance at Leroy.

"Damn," Leroy whispered, checking his handheld energy recorders. Leroy eased over to the far side of the room while he continued to shoot video at the same time.

Several scenarios ran through my mind as to what to do next. I wasn't sure if Chauncey was awake and aware, or if perhaps he was sleepwalking.

"Who are you?" Chauncey demanded, as the lights flickered and flashed in random patterns and the temperature continued to drop.

"I'm Amanda." I stepped closer. "Your brother, Philippe invited me to the house."

"My brother is Claude." He flicked a hand in annoyance. "You make no sense. Leave me." And with those words he dismissed us and went back to staring at the portrait once again.

"You're not Chauncey," I said, and my heart began to race with excitement.

He didn't bother to look my way. "No. I am not."

"Who are you?" I asked. I needed to be sure. God knows there were plenty of spirits in this house.

He turned slowly around. "Pierre-Michel Marquette." He introduced himself, even as his eyes raked up and down my body. "You're dressed oddly for a woman. How did you get in here?" He shifted and regarded Leroy as he stood there filming the encounter. The possessed man shook his head as if confused. "Are you both servants?"

I'd met Chauncey once before at the Grand Opening. He'd been polite and charming, nothing like he was acting tonight...The emotion radiating from him was intensely negative and I felt it hit me square in the chest. Easing slightly off to one side to lessen the impact, I saw the reason for my revulsion.

There was a faint arc of energy going from the painting and into Chauncey's back. *The painting was the conduit,* I realized. Sweat had popped out on his brow. Chauncey was fighting the spirit, but Pierre-Michel was determined.

"Are you recording that energy arc?" I said under my breath to Leroy, as the man before us began to pace back and forth and swear, in French.

"I am." Leroy's voice was soft. "The equipment is going nuts. I've never seen paranormal energy register so high."

"We have to get him away from that

portrait." My voice was quiet, but it was as if we weren't even in the room.

"Chauncey?" Estella stepped into the room despite my warning.

I shot out an arm to keep her back. "That's not Chauncey," I said

"What's wrong with him?" Estella whispered. "He's not even dressed."

"Spirit possession." I swallowed back my concern and tried to remain dispassionate and analytical. I'd seen a lot of things over the years, but I'd only witnessed a spirit possessing someone to this degree once before. Chauncey became more agitated, and his motions were stiff and jerky. He was fighting the spirit who had taken possession of him. The longer this episode went on the more damage it would inflict upon the host.

"What do we do?" Estella asked me.

"Find out why Pierre-Michel is here." I nudged her back. "Please let me handle this."

"Be careful," Leroy said, and moved over to stand in front of Estella.

I took a deep breath and focused on the entity and the man in front of us. "Pierre-Michel

Marquette, why are you here in this time and place? Is this about Bridgette?"

"Bridgette? No." He frowned. "I have to set things right."

I made sure to keep my voice low and calm. "What happened to her? How did she die?"

Chauncey's body began to shake. As we watched, another, younger face became superimposed over his. "She...fell into the water." The words were torn out of him. "I couldn't save her."

"Did you try?" That comment was from Estella, and it infuriated Pierre-Michel.

"I am *not* a killer!" All the overhead lights in the room exploded. The rage of the spirit had sent sparks and shards of glass from the broken bulbs raining down on all of us.

Even as Leroy and Estella ducked, I remained where I was, sizing up my opponent.

"It was an accident. I am innocent!" The voice of the spirit was deep as if layered and amplified. Out of the corner of my eye, I saw Estella clap her hands over her ears.

I'd had enough. There would be no reasoning with Pierre-Michel. This had to end quickly.

The physical effect of the prolonged possession on Chauncey would be brutal. "Pierre-Michel Marquette," I spoke his full name with intention. "I banish you!"

"There is something you must know," the spirit cried. "It was a lie! You are *mine*. Not hers!"

A spectral wind began to howl inside the room, and I stood firm against it. "This ends now," I said, raising my arms and my personal power at the same time.

Speaking the words my father had taught me, I began the magick that would send the spirit back to the other side of the veil. I bent my arms at the elbow, crossing my wrists in front of my face. As I began to chant, the power of the runes inside the cuffs of my jacket flared to life.

"Holy shit." I heard Estella's awed voice from behind me as Chauncey's body began to convulse and he was pulled up to his toes by the power of my magick.

I bore down and concentrated on the task at hand. The ghostly wind continued to shriek, but I would not be distracted from my purpose.

"Pierre-Michel Marquette I banish your spirit!" I shouted over the noise.

In answer, Chauncey's head was thrown back and his entire body arched backwards. The spirit continued to fight me, screaming in protest. I stayed in position, focusing on my opponent. I couldn't fail.

All around me glass cases shattered, yet I pressed on. Ignoring the sweat that ran down my back I pushed my magick out with everything I had. I felt the spirit begin to loosen its grip and took immediate advantage of the small victory. The spirit had put up a hell of a fight, but nevertheless, it was fading.

Everything seemed to freeze. Particles of glass flying through the air shimmered as if they were suspended in time. Sparks from the remains of the overhead lights stopped in their fall to the ground, but most importantly, the eerie arcs of energy that were attaching Chauncey to the portrait had ceased.

I saw it all in that spilt-second as if I was viewing the scene from above. Myself, holding the pose and braced against the onslaught of power from the spirit... Estella and Leroy just off to my left fighting to stay on their feet. Chauncey, his body drawn impossibly tight and arched back from the angry spirit possessing his body...and then...Deputy Zakary Parker rushing into the room with his gun drawn.

"Sherriff's department!" he shouted.

This was the moment. No matter what, it had to be now. Zakary's arrival was inconsequential to the task at hand. With the final words of the incantation I yanked my crossed arms apart and sent the spirit back to the other side.

Instantly time sped back up. With the deafening boom of a thunderclap, the force of the energy I'd expended sent all of the glass fragments flying back in the opposite direction. The displacement of energy had the walls shaking and my ears ringing.

Slowly I lowered my arms and checked on the people around me. Leroy was helping Estella to her feet, Chauncey was swaying on his, and Zakary was sitting back up from out in the hallway. He'd been blown backwards and out of the room by the force of so much energy leaving the physical plane.

"So mote it be," I said, and shook out my

hands.

There was a moment of silence, and then Chauncey Marquette's eyes rolled up in his head. With a little moan, he crumbled.

"Chauncey!" Estella sprang past me and managed to catch him before his head bounced off the floor.

"What in the fuck just happened in here?" Zakary demanded. He stomped back into the room, and grabbed me by the elbow. "Amanda, what did you do?"

He'd seen everything. There would be no going back to the role of the quiet librarian with Zakary now. However, at the moment my main concern was the pale, bleeding man sprawled out in front of me.

"I need to check on Chauncey," I said, removing his hand from my elbow.

Leroy stepped in. "Give her a minute, Parker."

Zakary put his gun back in his holster. "You have two minutes." His voice was flat and angry.

"I'm going to get the main lights back on," Leroy announced and left to do so.

"Thanks, Leroy." I blew out a breath and went to check on Chauncey Marquette.

The man lay unconscious in Estella's arms. "He's bleeding," she said.

"Let me see him," I said, kneeling down.

Estella pulled him closer. "I can't see him well enough to know how badly he's hurt."

A flashlight clicked on and Zakary aimed the beam on the unconscious man. "Here, this will help."

"Thank you," I said, reaching to check the pulse at his throat. I found it to be far too fast. Chauncey was not responding to Estella calling his name, and his breathing was labored. There were dozens of nicks and cuts from the flying glass across his chest and arms. Most concerning to me however, was how cold he felt.

"Do you want me to call for an ambulance?" Zakary asked.

"Maybe. Give me a moment to see what I can do, first." I answered without looking back at the deputy.

"What can we do to help him?" Estella asked me.

"We need to get him warmed up," I told Estella, and unzipped my jacket. I shrugged out of it and shards of glass fell to the floor. Quickly, I shook it out, and draped it across his naked chest. No sooner had I covered him when the lights in the mansion all came back on.

Behind me I heard a gasp of surprise and I didn't bother to look for the reason of Zakary's reaction. With my hair up, and in the lace camisole, most of the sacred tattoos and glyphs were visible.

At the moment, my main concern was for the victim of the possession. With that thought in mind, I put my hands on either side of Chauncey's face, and began to chant a healing charm.

"What are you doing?" Zakary asked, his tone suspicious.

"She's doing healing work," Estella said, and after a few repetitions, she joined in.

By the time Leroy arrived a few minutes later, Chauncey had begun to stir.

"Chauncey?" Estella gave his arms a squeeze, and I lifted my hands from him. "Hey," she said. "Can you hear me?"

His eyes fluttered and slowly he opened them. "Estella?" He focused on the woman who held him so protectively.

"There you are." She blew out a long breath and dropped her forehead to his.

"How are you feeling Mr. Marquette?" I asked briskly.

"Strange." He blinked a few times. "Where am I?"

"You're in the museum room at the main house," I said.

He frowned. "How in the hell did I get over here?"

"You don't remember?" I asked. His pupils were very large, and his skin was still too cool. He was in shock.

"No," he said. "The last thing I recall was lying on the couch in my apartment watching television."

Estella pulled him closer. "Maybe we should take him to the hospital."

"No," he said, trying to sit up. "I'm all right."

Estella tightened her grip. "You stay down Marquette, until Amanda says you're okay to get up."

"Deputy," I said calmly, "if you would be so kind as to call for an ambulance for Mr. Marquette. I think he needs to be seen at the ER."

Zakary reached for the speaker at his shoulder and called it in.

Chauncey lifted the jacket that was draped over him and frowned down at the cuts across his bare chest. "What happened to me? I'm all cut up. Did I fall through a window or something?" He looked around at the room and saw the broken glass from the shattered display cases. "What happened in here?"

"That's what I want to know." Zakary glared at me.

"First things first. Let's get Mr. Marquette taken care of, and afterwards I'll be happy to answer any questions you may have."

Zakary's eyes bore furiously into mine. "Damn right you will."

***

Estella and Zakary helped Chauncey, and together they moved him to a club chair in the eastern lobby. Estella ran up to the family wing to go and fetch Chauncey a blanket then sat beside him while they waited for the emergency services to arrive.

Chauncey grumbled about the ambulance, but he was weak enough that it was a token protest at best. I had promised to contact Philippe if there were any problems, and this certainly qualified as one. He beat the ambulance up to the house by five minutes. Which wasn't surprising as the EMS unit had to come from Alton which was twenty miles down the river road, while the farmhouse was only a few miles away.

The deputy stood back silently but listened intently to every conversation going on around him. I briefly explained to Philippe what had happened, and Leroy added in his perspective as he broke down his equipment.

Estella was solely focused on Chauncey, and her behavior had me wondering about the pair of them. She was quietly razzing him as they waited for the ambulance and it kept Chauncey smiling, even though he was shivering so much that his teeth were chattering.

Once Chauncey was on his way to the hospital, with his brother and Estella following in Philippe's car, Leroy began to stack all the equipment cases by the door.

"Deputy?" I gestured for Zakary to follow me and strode straight into a conference room off the eastern lobby.

Walking over to the table, I draped my jacket across a chair, and took a seat. I was exhausted from performing both the banishing and the healing work required to minimize Chauncey's injuries. Closing my eyes, I tried to ground and center my own energy, and blew out a slow breath, bracing myself for the conversation that was about to occur.

CHAPTER SEVEN

Zakary stalked into the conference room and shut the door firmly behind him. "I want some answers, Amanda."

I opened my eyes, and for the first time since he'd barged in during the banishing ritual, I looked him straight in the face. "I imagine you do."

I tried to focus on him, and discovered that he was blurry. I realized, belatedly, that my glasses were smeared and smudged. With a sigh, I pulled them off and wiped the lenses clean on the hem of my camisole. I couldn't see him clearly from across the room without my glasses on, but I could tell that he was staring at me. The deputy had gone stock still like he'd never seen me before.

"My god." His voice was ragged.

I slipped the glasses back on. "Where would you like to begin?"

"What was that *thing* you did back there?" He lifted up his arms in a similar position to the one I'd used. "What was that?"

"Magick," I said.

"Wait, *what*?" he croaked.

"Magick," I repeated.

"I don't understand." He mimicked the pose again. "That's not magick."

"The gesture you are so crudely trying to duplicate is *useless* without the knowledge and skill required to back it up," I said. "Contrary to what many people believe it is not simply the gesture that holds the magick. It is in fact, the understanding of how to wield the power, and the magician's personal strength that banishes a spirit."

"Banishes a spirit..." His voice trailed off, and he shook his head as if to clear it. "Don't play games with me! What exactly did I just walk in on?"

I folded my hands on the table. "What do *you* think you walked in on?"

"Answering a question with another question is considered an evasive tactic."

I inclined my head. "Maieutic," I said. "It's referred to correctly as *maieutic*. That's the method of answering questions with questions in order for the questioner to understand he can find the answer by reasoning it out for himsel —"

I cut myself off when Zakary growled in frustration. "I apologize," I said contritely.

"For what exactly?" he shot back.

"I'm sorry that you are upset. I'm sorry that you had to witness that. I'm sure for a layman the event was quite upsetting—frightening even."

"I didn't say I was afraid." Zakary scowled. "But I do want to know exactly what it was that I saw. Was that a demon or something?"

"It was a spirit. The spirit of Pierre-Michel Marquette to be exact."

He narrowed his eyes. "You mean the guy who murdered his wife back in the 1840's?"

"I don't think that he did murder her."

"And why is that?"

"Didn't you hear him, before you burst in?" I

folded my arms on the table. "By the way, why are you even here, Deputy?"

"We received a call. Suspicious cars at the winery after hours."

"Neither you or the caller recognized the Midnight family truck?"

Zakary waved that away. "I pulled up, heard this god-awful noise, and saw the lights flashing up at the mansion, so I went in."

"Of course you did," I sighed.

Zakary pointed at me. "Let's stay on subject here."

"What subject are you referring to exactly?" I asked

"Is it gone—the ghost or spirit?"

I sighed again. "For now."

"Where did it go?"

"Back through the portal I believe."

"So what I saw, was what...like an exorcism?"

"No." I gave him a small smile. "I'm not a priest, Zakary. I don't perform exorcisms."

"Oh, good! I'm not dating a priest!" He drug a hand through his hair. "Boy, would *that* have been awkward trying to explain to my mother."

His laugh was bitter. "Here I thought I was dating such a nice girl. A super smart, classy, pretty librarian..."

"I *am* a librarian," I interrupted him.

"You're a hell of a lot more than a librarian!" Zakary stopped, and spun on his heel. "What *are* you?"

"I'm the same woman you've been dating for the past six weeks—"

"The hell you are!" he shot back. "You may talk like her, but you don't even look like my Amanda. All of the sudden you're covered in tattoos!"

He'd said, *my Amanda*. Which was a telling moment. It made me wonder if I would ever hear him say that again. Knowing that I needed to remain calm, I took a deep breath. "As to the tattoos, they're not a new addition. I've had them for years, Zakary. You've simply never seen them before."

He crossed his arms and studied me. "I'm looking at you, and I don't know what to think. You sit there with perfect posture, your hair up, and in those purple glasses...all prim and proper, but from the neck down you look like a biker chick. You're actually wearing a black lace camisole—I can see your bra! And you've got on ripped jeans."

I tried a smile. "You don't approve of casual clothing?"

"Knock it off. You know what I mean. I honestly don't know how I feel about the ink..." he trailed off.

"Do the tattoos upset you?" I reached behind me for my jacket.

He reached out as if to stop me. "No, they don't *upset* me. But...I have to ask. Are those all occult symbols?"

I left the jacket where it was. "That would be correct," I said evenly.

"Jesus!" He shook his head. "I feel like I'm in the god damn *Twilight Zone*, or something..."

"Perhaps you should sit down." I gestured to a chair at the table.

"Maybe I should." With a half laugh, Zakary took a seat across from me.

Not next to me, I noted. Instead he kept the table *between* us. Lines had been drawn.

Zakary sat there, his once open and handsome face had shifted into solemn lines.

His blue eyes were serious and unsmiling, and he was watching me very closely, as if he were waiting for me to speak—or to confess.

"I'm trying to decide where to best begin," I admitted after a moment.

He rested his arms on the table. "You can start with why you kept this part of your life a secret."

I cleared my throat. "In addition to my full-time position at the library, I also have...I suppose you could say...a secondary job."

"Secondary job?" His brows went way up.

Silently, I cursed my poor choice of words. "An *avocation,* would perhaps be a better depiction."

He leaned forward. "You're telling me that you have a *job* working with spooky and weird stuff?"

"The correct terminology would in fact be, 'the paranormal'."

"Fine," he said. "You have a profession that deals with things that go bump in the night. So you're like a ghost hunter or something?"

"I've been called a hunter before and that's accurate to a certain extent. I only deal with the more severe cases, or disturbances, you might say."

"Still you chose to keep your *cases* a secret from me," he said. "Why didn't you tell me about this other part of your life?"

My hair was falling out of the pins. I reached back and quickly pulled them out, and scrubbed a hand through the back of my hair. While I tucked the bobby pins in my jeans pocket I considered how much I could safely tell him. "Very few people know about this, Zakary, and that is *deliberate*. I'm sorry if your feelings are hurt over the omission. However, this particular calling has been kept secret for generations."

"Generations?" he frowned. "Does your family know about your hobby?"

"Yes, they know, and let me be crystal clear, Zakary. This is *not* a hobby."

His eyes held mine. "So you're serious about all of this paranormal stuff?"

Even though the word *stuff* rankled, I coolly inclined my head. "Yes, I am very serious."

"I can't believe this!" he said. "Your father had a hand in training me when I was a rookie. He was very well respected at the station. I find it hard to believe that Victor would be on board with any of this."

It took everything I had not to snap back that my father had in fact, trained *me* to take over for him. Instead, I concentrated on keeping my own emotions under control. "Yes," I said, "I am aware that my father trained you before he retired."

"And your family?" Zakary's eyes were huge. "They're okay with your...er...*interests*?"

Before I could answer, there was a knock on the door and Leroy poked his head in. "Excuse me." His voice matched his facial expression: pleasant. "I'm almost finished packing up the equipment, Mandy."

"Thank you, Leroy. I'll be out to help you carry it to the car, shortly."

"And you." Zakary spun in his chair to glare at Leroy. "You're in on this game as well?"

Leroy's face hardened. "Son, I understand that you may be having a hard time wrapping your mind around what you witnessed tonight, but don't push me."

I tried to intervene, "Leroy—"

"Be quiet, Mandy," Leroy said gently,

stepping fully into the room. "How long are you going to sit here and let him interrogate you? You don't owe the deputy anything."

Zakary rose to his feet. "We'll see how far that attitude takes you when I haul the both of you down to the station for further questioning."

Leroy laughed. "On what charge?"

"Breaking and entering, for starters," Zakary argued. "I imagine I could get destruction of property or vandalism to stick."

"I'd like to point out that we had permission from the homeowner to be here tonight," I said in an attempt to keep the peace.

I shouldn't have bothered. The men were almost toe to toe.

Leroy got right in Zakary's face. "If you'd pull your head out of your ass for two seconds, Deputy, maybe you'd remember that Philippe Marquette was the first person Mandy called after Chauncey was injured."

"Step back, Mr. Holtgrave," Zakary growled.

"We didn't cause the damage to the museum room, Zakary," I said, keeping my voice quiet.

"What in the hell did?" he demanded.

"The spirit," I said. "Call it an entity or a ghost, it was angry enough to have manifested corporeal damage on the physical plane."

"Sweet Jesus." Zakary rubbed both hands over his face. "Corporeal damage...I can't believe I'm having this conversation."

"For the love of god," Leroy grumbled, taking his cell phone from his pocket. "I'm gonna pull rank on your ass, boy."

Zakary glared at Leroy. "Who are you calling, *boy*?"

"As lovely as this has been, I do believe we're finished for the night." I stood up and shrugged my jacket on, while Leroy spoke to someone on his cell.

"No, we're *not* finished!" Zakary argued. "Not by a long shot."

I zipped my jacket closed and immediately felt stronger and more in control. "Unless you were serious about charging us with a crime...Then, *yes,* Deputy, we are finished." I pulled my hair out from the collar of my jacket and began to walk out of the room.

Zakary immediately moved between me and the doorway. "You can't seriously drop a bomb like this and expect me to just let things go?"

I was standing directly in front of him now, and as I searched his face I saw several emotions pass over it: disbelief, betrayal and anger were a few. Because of that, I tried one more time. "In a few days, after you've had a chance to think things over, why don't you contact me and we can discuss the matter more?"

"There's no way I'm letting you walk out of here tonight until you explain yourself to my satisfaction," Zakary said.

"Deputy Parker." Leroy's voice was firm. "The Sherriff would like a word with you." Leroy held out his cell phone.

Zakary took it. "Sir?" he began, "We have a situation—" and he suddenly fell silent, listening to his supervisor.

I didn't have to know exactly what was said. The look on the deputy's face was enough.

"Yes, sir," he finally said. "I see. Thank you, sir." He handed the phone back to Leroy.

Leroy smirked at him. "You can leave now, Deputy. Mandy and I need to load up the equipment and lock the house before we go."

Zakary glared at me for a long moment. He opened his mouth as if to speak, then shut it. Turning on his heel, he left without another word.

Leroy and I waited until we heard the door to the private entrance slam shut. Once it did and we were alone, I blew out a long breath, allowing my shoulders to drop.

"Ha!" Leroy said, holding the conference room door open for me. "Boy doesn't know who he's messing with."

"I sincerely appreciate Randall's help," I said, speaking of the Sherriff. "Especially tonight."

Together the two of us walked to the lobby. I gathered up my personal items as Leroy double checked that he had everything.

"Old Randall and me, we go way back," Leroy said, snapping the locks on the last equipment cases.

Almost everything was stacked neatly by the door and I was more than ready to go home. "I'm glad you thought to call him," I said to Leroy. "I think his intervention helped defuse the situation with the deputy."

I picked up one of the cases and followed Leroy outside. We made several trips back and forth to load it all up. Leroy was very excited to get home and start going over the data he'd gathered. I listened to him, doing my best *not* to think about Zakary's reaction to what he'd walked in on.

While Leroy enthusiastically talked about his calculations and readings, I locked the door to the mansion and put in the temporary security code Philippe had given us.

"Oh yeah," Leroy said as he popped the door locks on his sedan. "The Sherriff says if you don't have anywhere else to be on Thanksgiving, he'd like you to come and eat with his family."

I hit the remote start on my car to let it warm up and walked to my car, shivering in the cold wind that whipped across the cliffs. "That's very generous, I'll call him tomorrow."

"Since I'm going to be at my daughter's house in St. Louis, then I drive—"

"Down to Texas to visit your son's family for a few weeks. I remember."

"Anyway, you should definitely join the

Randalls. I don't like the thought of you being alone on the holidays."

"Don't worry about me, Leroy. I'm fine."

"I'll call you tomorrow and check in, anyway. G'night, Mandy." Leroy gave a wave and drove off.

I climbed in my car and let my head fall back against the head rest. If I wouldn't have been drained from the work tonight I might have had the energy to cry. I almost wished I did. Instead I felt hollow. I played the discussion in the conference room over in my mind, and cringed at how poorly it had gone.

As I drove home I had to wonder what would infuriate Zakary more? Discovering my secrets? The Sherriff who knew about our paranormal work—but hadn't told him. Being told to stop with his harassment of us? *Or* the fact that the Sherriff was also my godfather.

This was bad. Worse than I had imagined. I had no idea what would happen the next time I saw the deputy. But for now, I would give him some space.

I would deal with the inevitable fallout whenever it came.

***

The next week passed quietly. Chauncey Marquette had been released from the hospital the morning after the possession. Leroy and I met to go over the footage he'd captured that night at the mansion, and it was impressive. After carefully considering our options, we invited Philippe Marquette to view the footage as well. I also had the unpleasant task of informing Philippe that the portrait of his ancestor should be destroyed. I carefully explained that the painting was acting as a gateway for the spirit to travel back and forth to the physical world.

That gateway needed to be closed once and for all.

Philippe wasn't happy with that suggestion, but he did allow me to remove the portrait from the mansion for the time being. At the moment it was being stored inside a large, salt filled wooden crate in my cellar. I'd taken further steps to shut the portal down, and had surrounded the box with sacred herbs, stones, and magickal seals that I'd drawn all over the box.

Once Pierre-Michel's ghost had been put in the magickal equivalent of a time out, I went to visit Chauncey at his carriage-house apartment to see how he was recovering from the possession. Even though Gabriella was more than capable of tending to any psychic injuries, I still wanted to check on the man myself. I knocked on his door and was very surprised when Estella answered.

"Hey, Amanda." Estella grinned at me.

"Estella, I didn't expect to find you here."

She pulled the door open and motioned for me to come inside. "It was my turn to babysit."

"Oh?" I raised my eyebrows as I stepped inside. "Is someone not being a very good patient?"

"You got that right." Estella rolled her eyes. "So I volunteered to kick his stubborn ass up to the line."

"I heard that." Chauncey's voice came from the back. "Stop nagging me, woman."

Estella tossed a glare over her shoulder. "Well I wouldn't nag if you'd rest and let your body heal."

Chauncey walked out of a back room and was limping heavily. I assumed he'd exited the bathroom as his hair was wet, he wore a pair of sweats and had a towel draped around his neck. He carried a t-shirt in one hand and a first aid kit in the other. "Hello Amanda." He nodded. "I'm glad you stopped by. I wanted to speak with you."

"Chauncey," I said, giving him a polite smile. "I came to check in, and see how you're recovering after the other night."

"He overdid it today," Estella said before Chauncey could respond.

"I'm not an invalid," Chauncey grumbled.

"Sit down." Estella's voice was firm even as she guided him to a chair. "Let me put some fresh bandages on those cuts."

Instead of arguing, Chauncey sat slowly in an overstuffed recliner. "I don't understand why I'm so sore. It feels like someone beat the hell out of me."

"Estella," I said, as she hovered nervously over the man. "Why don't you put on a pot of tea, and Chauncey and I can have a talk about how best to recover from a psychic attack."

Estella frowned, but gave in. "Fine. Maybe you can talk some sense into the *pendejo*."

I sat on the sofa across from Chauncey. "I'll do my best."

"Humph." Estella stomped off into the adjoining kitchen and started rooting through the cupboards looking for the tea.

"The tea is in the blue tin on the counter," Chauncey called over. He closed his eyes and let his head fall back against the cushions.

I ran my eyes over his chest and saw that while the majority of the lacerations were minor, he had ended up getting a few stitches in places from the flying glass. He still had circles under his eyes as well, and even with a brief assessment I could see that his personal energy had been drained.

"With your permission, Chauncey," I said, briskly, "I'd like to do some healing work on you to help you regain your strength."

His eyes fluttered open. "You did something like that on me the other night, didn't you?"

"Yes, I did."

"I thought I remembered that," he said.

"Philippe and Estella filled me in on what happened, but I'd like to hear about it from your perspective."

I felt sympathy for the man. He looked like he'd been hit by a truck, and I knew from personal experience just how debilitating a psychic attack could be. "First things first," I said. "Let's get more fluids into you."

"Told you." Estella's smug voice came from the kitchen.

"Do you have any sports type drinks here?" I asked.

"He does," she answered for him. Estella reached in the fridge, pull out a bottle of orange sports drink. "Heads up," she said, and tossed it across the apartment.

"Thanks." I snagged the plastic bottle with one hand.

"Nice catch." Estella smiled and went back to filling up the tea kettle.

I twisted off the top and handed it to him. "Drink it all. The electrolytes and sugar will help you feel better."

"I'm too damn tired to argue." Chauncey shrugged and started to drain the bottle.

I raised my eyebrows. "You didn't have to chug it."

He finished the drink and set the empty bottle aside. "I'll confess, I've been feeling very weak and shaky since Sunday night."

"Did you just admit to being less than perfect?" Estella said from the kitchen. "*Dios mío*! You must be feeling bad."

I ignored the snarky comments from my friend. "When you've been attacked by negative energy, the recovery process makes one feel as if they are getting over the flu."

Chauncey nodded. "Yes. That's it exactly. "I'm hungry but food doesn't appeal. I feel very achy and fatigued."

I moved around to the back of the recliner and gently rested my fingertips on his shoulders. "Okay?" I asked, making sure he was all right with hands-on healing.

"Sure," he said tipping his head back to meet my eyes. "At this point I'm willing to try anything."

"This won't take long," I said, pressing my hands carefully down on the tops of his shoulders. "Try and relax." I made sure to avoid hitting the stitches at his collarbone area and silently transferred a bit of my own personal energy into him.

"Wow, your hands are suddenly very warm," he said.

"Breathe," I told him. "Take some nice deep breaths. Pull in clean white healing light when you inhale, hold it, and now exhale...releasing any negativity."

Chauncey did as I directed, and after a couple of minutes I shut down the energy I'd transferred over to him. I blew out a long breath myself, lifted my hands, and shook off the residual. "Feel better?" I asked, moving around to stand in front of him.

"Yes, actually I do." He smiled. "Much better. Thank you, Amanda."

"In another few days, with plenty of rest, and fluids, you'll be as good as new," I promised.

"The tea is steeping," Estella announced, returning to the living room. She snatched the first aid kit from the arm of Chauncey's chair. "If Amanda is done with her mo-jo, let's get you patched back up."

Chauncey managed to send Estella a

withering look. "I'm perfectly capable of slapping a few adhesive bandages over my stitches, Estella."

Estella opened the box and pulled out a tube of antibiotic cream. "Yeah, yeah...you're *muy macho*. I'm still going to help you. So just quit your bitchin'."

"You're just looking for any excuse to get your hands on my body again, admit it." Chauncey teased her.

I watched as Estella fumbled with the bandages. She recovered quickly, but I'd seen her involuntary reaction to his playful words.

"Oh well, damn it," she said, mildly. "You've seen through my clever ruse." She fluttered her lashes. "I get *so* turned on by ointment, bandages, and injured men."

Chauncey snorted with laughter over her banter, and I wondered again about the two of them. There was some definite chemistry in the air...and while Estella 'patched him back up', I wisely refrained from commenting, and instead went and poured the tea.

CHAPTER EIGHT

Normally my kitchen was a place of refuge. A sanctuary against the forces of evil and protection from any village drama or paranormal intrigue that lurked outside...

The afternoon before Thanksgiving however, I found myself squared off against a rather formidable opponent, and inside my very own home no less. Estella Flores Midnight was on a roll, in a temper, and quite frankly, I would have preferred dealing with a demonic entity.

She stood with her hands on her hips, and she was shouting. "What do you mean, you're staying home *alone* tomorrow?"

"Estella." I kept my voice low hoping she would clue in and lower hers. "For the third time, it's fine." I pointed to the Cornish game hen thawing on the counter. "I plan to roast a chicken, and to enjoy a quiet day off."

"Being by yourself on the holidays totally sucks," Estella argued. "I should know. I spent the last several alone."

"Estella, this is my choice. I was invited to have dinner with the Randalls, but I passed on their invitation because I'd *prefer* to stay here instead. It'll be relaxing, and it will give me a chance to get started on my decorating for the holidays."

"I call bullshit." Estella tossed her head. "I think you're staying here because you're worried you will run into the deputy. You're hiding."

I sighed. The truth was that if I went to dinner at Sherriff Randall's home—there would be a better than average chance of bumping into Zakary. Sherriff Randall's wife had an open-door policy with the staff at the department. More often than not, they dropped by his house to visit, or to grab a meal to go if they were on shift.

There was no way I'd get a last-minute flight to Florida to spend Thanksgiving with my parents, I tried. The only seats left on flights to Florida were astronomically expensive—far beyond my current budget. Therefore, as discretion was the better part of valor, I chose the safe route and opted to spend Thanksgiving by myself.

Trying to convince my young friend of the wisdom in that decision was quite another matter.

Estella crossed her arms. "If you think I'm going to let you sit here alone so you can sulk, you've got another thing coming."

Nyx pranced into the kitchen and head-butted Estella's ankles. "Meow," she cried, and with a flip of her tail, she sat next to Estella.

I glared at the traitorous feline. "Forgetting who feeds you?" I asked the cat.

Nyx's answer was a deep purr as she rubbed her face against Estella's boots.

"See?" Estella laughed. "Even the cat is on my side. You should come and have dinner with your family."

"They don't even have any idea that we're related," I reminded her.

"Maybe it's time to tell them."

"No," I said, immediately. "It's not."

"Why the hell not?" She wanted to know. "I'm not saying you should spill the beans about the Guardian thing, but I do think you should tell the family that you are our cousin."

"Would you believe me if I told you that I'll *know* when it's time?" I pressed a hand to my stomach. "My gut tells me it's not time yet, I try to listen to my intuition whenever possible. Especially for something as important as this."

"You kept the whole Guardian thing from the deputy and that secret ended up biting you in the ass," Estella pointed out. "Are you sure you're not stalling because you're worried about being rejected again?"

Deliberately, I gave myself a moment before answering. "I am not afraid of being rejected by the Midnights, Estella. What I *am* concerned about is now more people are aware of my role as a Guardian than ever before."

"So?"

"It puts you all at risk." I tried to make her understand. Leroy knows exactly what the job entails. Gabriella understands to a certain degree—"

"Hey, I had a ringside seat." Estella nodded. "Trust me, you made a hell of an impression on me."

I tried to finish my sentence. "Be that as it may, now the deputy, you, *and* your sister all know my identity. And if anything were to happen—"

"You'd feel responsible." Estella finished.

"I *would* be responsible."

"But still you let me go with you the other night," Estella argued.

"Yes, I did." I folded my own arms, mirroring her pose. "I allowed you to be there because I felt after everything you'd been through, you deserved to see the haunting come to an end."

"You've got his ghost locked up good and tight?" Estella's voice was brisk, but her eyes gave away her concern.

"Yes, the spirit is contained," I promised. "He's not going anywhere."

"Where is he?" Estella asked.

"Somewhere safe." I left it at that. No one, not even Leroy knew that the portrait was currently locked up in a hidden room in my cellar.

"Come to dinner with the family," Estella urged me. "After everything you've done to help with the crazy ghosts, you should be there."

I gave an exaggerated sigh. "Does anyone *ever* win an argument with you?"

"Nope." Estella grinned. "Besides, if things go on too long, I just put them in a headlock and wait until they pass out. It makes folks much easier to manage."

***

I did end up celebrating Thanksgiving with the Midnights and the Marquettes. I was informed that the family was going to gather at Drusilla and Garrett Rivers' home, and I was relieved to hear that the holiday wasn't being celebrated at the Marquette mansion after my last encounter there.

I told myself it was an excellent opportunity to get to know the Marquette and Midnight families better, *and* to see how Chauncey was recovering. Besides, I'd always wanted to see the renovations to Garrett Rivers' historic home.

I pulled up in front of the Italianate brick house and parked my car. I flipped down the rearview mirror and checked my appearance one last time. The plum sweater was a good choice. It complimented the dusty purple frames of my glasses and turned my eyes a brighter shade of green. I'd worn my hair down in loose curls over my shoulders today, and the style made me look softer and more approachable.

I reached over and picked up the pumpkin pie I'd brought along and headed for the front door. My low-heeled gray boots clicked against the limestone walkway and I admired the chrysanthemums that were still blooming in bronze and orange colors in the flower beds on either side of the small porch.

I knocked on the red door, and was greeted by both Estella and Brooke James, Garrett's young ward. I passed off the pie to the girl, who took off with it straight away. Estella took my coat and tossed it on a bench in the foyer.

"I'm glad you're here," Estella said. She

looped her arm through mine and steered me back through the house to a large, albeit noisy kitchen filled with people. As one they all said hello.

"Hello everyone." I smiled. "Thank you for inviting me to dinner."

Priscilla Midnight, the family matriarch, was sitting at the kitchen table beginning to show Brooke how to put a salad together. Nicole Dubois was mashing potatoes in a large pot at the counter. Gabriella was stirring something in a saucepan on top of the stove, and Garrett was helping Drusilla pull a gorgeous roasted turkey out of the oven.

Estella offered to get me a glass of wine, so I ducked out of the kitchen and followed her into a handsome room with a leather sofa and chairs. The walls were deep green trimmed in dark wood, and an exquisite antique family heraldry hung above the fireplace.

My breath caught at seeing Melusine, the two tailed mermaid. Some legends claimed that she was a faerie, or a Siren. Others insisted she was a goddess...but either way, the Rivers family name just took on a new level of importance.

I sat on the couch and sipped at my wine, and wondered over this new development.

Seemingly oblivious to the goddess on the wall above, Philippe, Max Dubois, Jacob Ames, and Chauncey watched a football game on the wide screen television. The men were arguing over the ability of the offensive line, and Max held his six-month-old son on his lap. Danielle sat on the carpet and Jaime Ames was next to her, building towers out of wooden blocks.

Danielle let loose a belly laugh when she knocked over a stack. Which made Jaime determined to build the blocks up faster. I sat back on the couch and tried to get my shoulders to unclench. Camilla strolled in, dropped a loud kiss on Jaime's blonde head and joined us on the sofa.

Talk shifted to her wedding, which was taking place on the second Saturday of December. Estella rolled her eyes at her sister, calling her a Bridezilla. The comment had Camilla chuckling and teasing her sister about being a rookie bridesmaid.

"At least you didn't make me wear pink,"

Estella said, tossing back her wine.

"Oh, did I forget to mention that the shoes I ordered for you came in?" Camilla asked airily.

"Shoes?" Estella scowled.

"Yes," her sister said. "Shoes for you to wear with your bridesmaid dress."

"What's wrong with the black heels I already have?"

Camilla brushed at her bright pink hair. "The shoes I ordered compliment the theme of the wedding, you might say…" She waited a beat and then nudged her sister in the arm. "They're pink."

"Christ Jesus." Estella's jaw dropped. "You didn't."

"I did," Camilla said, laughing at Estella's horrified expression.

"I'm sure it will be lovely," I said in an attempt to be polite.

"God damn it." Estella stood up. "I gotta wear *pink* shoes? I definitely need another drink."

She stomped off to the bar that was set up across the room and I found myself alone with Camilla Midnight.

"Did you really order her pink shoes?" I couldn't resist asking.

"Guilty." Camilla grinned. "For all the bridesmaids. It's going to look fabulous. You'll see."

I bit my lip to keep from laughing over Estella being outmaneuvered by her sister. Brooke came in to introduce me to her cat, Tabby, while all around me conversations were happening at the same time.

I found myself with a lap full of cat, listening to Brooke's animated chatter about her current book report at school. The house was noisy and crowded with people. There were men cheering over the football game, and children playing happily on the floor. Camilla and Estella debated the importance of bridal party footwear, and down the hall the kitchen was a hive of activity.

It was not unlike being in the center of a three ringed circus. And for the first time in days, I found myself relaxing.

***

The second weekend in December arrived, and still there'd been no contact from the deputy. Privately I could admit to being hurt by that, but perhaps, it was better if things had never gone any further.

Still, I chose my dress for Camilla Midnight's wedding with great care. I knew that Zakary would also be at the wedding as he was friends with Jacob Ames, the groom. In fact, he was an usher. We'd talked about going together to the wedding back when we'd been dating, but that point was now moot.

I stood before my closet in full makeup with my hair done, wearing a black lace bra and matching panties, surveying my wardrobe. The formal evening ceremony and reception were being held in the main ballroom at the Marquette mansion. With only a few weeks left until Christmas, I imagined Camilla would do some type of holiday theme for her wedding.

I pulled out a vintage velvet navy blue dress. It was cut in the wrap-around style with a V neck. The sleeves fluttered to my elbows and the skirt was full. The hemline was long and asymmetrical, and after a careful check I discovered that I could still wear the slim thigh harness for my silver ritual blade.

The skirt fabric draped beautifully and concealed the harness well—which was one of the reasons I'd chosen the dress when I'd bought it. Carefully, I pulled the dress on and surveyed my reflection. The dark blue made the copper tones in my hair pop, and it was very flattering to my figure. I skipped wearing hose, and paired the dress with some strappy black shoes. I expected the shoes would kill my feet, but at least I'd look good while I suffered.

I selected a small clutch bag, added my wallet, phone, and a few tiny vials of potions— just in case. I also managed to squeeze my compact and a tube of lipstick in there as well. *Which,* I thought with a wry smile, *only showed where my priorities lay.* Blade and potions first, then if there was space, add the cosmetics.

I swirled a long coat over the dress and headed out the door. I stepped into the ceremony space a short time later, nodded to Nicole Dubois, and was greeted by Brooke James.

"Hi Amanda," she said, passing me a

program.

"Brooke, you look beautiful," I said, and it was true. The girl's ginger hair was curled down her back. She wore a pretty pink dress with a mock illusion neckline that was suitable for her age.

She smiled shyly in response to the compliment while I scanned the available seating. I spotted a likely chair near the side exit which would allow me to both discreetly observe *and* watch for any signs of trouble...paranormal or otherwise. I truly didn't expect for there to be any, not since I had the portrait safely contained, but it never hurt to err on the side of caution.

Directly ahead of me, Zakary was doing his duty as usher and escorting the female guests to their seats. In order to avoid any sort of confrontation, I threw a small glamour to cloak my movements, and started to ease into the back row on the bride's side as discreetly as possible.

"You're supposed to wait for an usher to seat you," Brooke stage whispered as I went down the back row.

"No worries." I tossed her a wink. "I'm fine."

Brooke returned to her attendant duties with a smile and I sat down in the last chair on the far end.

I opened my wedding program and pretended to be utterly fascinated by it. In other words, I used the program to block my face from Zakary's view as he went back and forth fulfilling his duties as usher.

After a few minutes, I realized I shouldn't have worried, either that or my glamour had worked very well. The deputy never even glanced my way. Telling myself it was ridiculous to be hurt by that after he'd ignored me for the past few weeks, I focused my attention on the decorations for the ceremony.

Pots of pink and white poinsettias lined the aisle. The long table where the officiant would stand was covered in a mixture of pink flowers and evergreen, with candles. Lots and lots of creamy white candles.

Brooke took her seat in the front row and the music changed. I watched as the groomsmen filed out to take their places up front. Next the groom began to escort his mother, Jenna, down the aisle with his father walking proudly off to the side and behind them.

The bridesmaids filed out and the daughters of Midnight looked fantastic. Gabriella, then Drusilla, and finally Estella walked down the aisle in pretty black dresses. The bridesmaid's gowns were knee-length in an A-line cut. Made of chiffon, they had an illusion neckline. Their flowers were pink carnations, white mums, and blush baby roses with sprigs of pine. I leaned forward to catch a glimpse of the dreaded shoes, and saw that they were pink stiletto pumps with a crisscrossing knot at the front. Like the dresses, they were stylish and subtly sexy.

Jacob's son Jaime came next looking bashful as the ring bearer. His outfit matched that of the groomsmen. A black suit, paired with a pale pink shirt and black tie. The music paused and everyone stood as the bride, Camilla, began to be escorted down the aisle by her grandmother.

Considering Camilla's hair color, and predilection for pink, I'd figured she would choose an edgy, hot pink dress. But I was pleasantly surprised by the chic ivory and blush-pink wedding gown. The bodice itself was cut in a deep V and made of a warm off-white lace. The sleeves were long and the skirt of the gown was in an A line silhouette, and made entirely of blush-pink tulle.

I saw that she carried a bouquet of pink roses, carnations, and white button mums. I spotted a touch of baby's breath in the bouquet and it gave the appearance of snow sprinkled over the bouquet. The effect was absolutely charming.

I sat back down in my chair, and the wedding began. That was when I saw Zakary standing on the opposite side of the room, staring at me.

I'd thought he'd been gorgeous in his Sheriff's department uniform, but the slim fitting suit displayed his build to a real advantage. *Damn the man for looking so good in that tux,* I thought. *It truly wasn't fair.* My stomach gave one hard twist as I recognized that I'd likely missed my chance to ever get my hands on him the way I'd dreamed of.

Let him go, I told myself. *Only a fool would keep looking that direction.* Resolutely, I shifted my gaze and returned my attention to the ceremony.

***

I'd managed to avoid any uncomfortable moments for the first hour or so of the reception. The ballroom was decorated in pink, ivory and silver ornaments, flocked evergreen branches, white lights, and more poinsettias. The room sparkled and shimmered somehow managing to hit the right balance between Christmas and bridal.

After dinner had been cleared away, the music was pumping, and the guests were partying. I was standing at the bar with Estella, who'd dared me into doing tequila shots with her. Considering the last time I'd been in that ballroom I'd had to play the damsel in distress, I decided to let my hair down—so to speak— and allow the true Amanda Beaumont a little breathing room.

I'd just slapped the empty shot glass down on the bar top in synch with Estella's, and was reaching for a lime wedge, when a familiar voice cut in.

"Tequila shots?" Zakary's voice was harsh and judgmental. "What's next, Amanda? Will you start dancing on the tables?"

"Possibly," I said, pitching my voice above the music. "But etiquette dictates that one must wait until *after* midnight to begin table-top dancing."

My snarky comment had Estella bursting out with laughter, while Zakary glared. "What game are you playing?" he demanded.

"Games?" I sucked on the lime and dropped it in the empty shot glass. "Deputy, I simply don't have the time or the inclination for such activities."

"I want to talk to you," he said. "Privately."

"How tragic." I shook my hair back. "This is hardly the place for a private conversation."

Over his shoulder I could see Estella grinning. She was enjoying this all way too much.

Zakary dropped a hand on my arm. "We can do this right here, or somewhere else. Your choice."

A few people had begun to stare, and I'd be

damned if I'd be the source of yet another scene at the Marquette mansion. "Estella?" I leaned around Zakary to meet her eyes. "I believe the deputy and I do need to clear the air, after all. Would you excuse us for a moment?"

"Sure." Estella's grin grew even wider. "Give 'em hell, honey."

"Deputy?" I inclined my head, regally. "Come with me, and we'll find somewhere less noisy to talk." Without looking to see if he would follow or not, I picked up my purse, and walked out of the ballroom.

I felt him more than I heard his footsteps because his angry energy was radiating against my back. The farther we traveled down the hall the less people we encountered. I looked for somewhere private, but stayed away from the museum room. Philippe had told me they were repairing the display cabinets and light fixtures. Besides, the door was probably locked anyway.

I took the stairs to the hotel suites and went straight up to the second floor landing. I paused, and heard voices, so that would never do. Decision made, I continued to the third floor. I passed the first guest room and stopped before I reached the second. I shifted to face him, my back against a wide window framed out by a cushioned window seat.

"This should allow for some privacy." I folded my hands over the purse and used my best librarian's tone of voice. "Now, Deputy, what did you want to talk to me about?"

He leaned in and got up in my face. I held my ground even as his eyes searched mine. "My god, how many women can you be?" he asked.

"As many as it takes to do my job," I said, before I thought better of it.

"Well, well. The truth at last." He eased back and took a breath, trying to compose himself. "You lie so well, Amanda, that it throws a man off when you're actually honest."

"I've never lied to you Zakary," I said, choosing my words carefully.

"Omission is a lie," he retorted. "You made me think you were someone you're not. You kept secrets from me."

"And I explained to you the reason for that —" I began.

"You let me believe you were shy and

inexperienced!" he interrupted. "You, whoever the hell you are, you're anything but. You played me for a fool."

"I never said I was inexperienced," I pointed out. "You simply assumed that since I didn't fall into bed with you after a few dates, that I must be."

"Then I see you doing tequila shots at the bar with Estella, and you're dressed like that!"

Now I was confused, *and* offended. "What does the type of alcohol I'm drinking have to do with anything?"

"You know what I mean." He snapped back.

"No, Deputy, I truly don't."

"Christ! Do you want me to spell it out for you?" He tossed his hands up in the air. "The town's librarian is at a fancy wedding, doing shots in a low-cut velvet dress? What will people say?"

"I don't give a fig what they say!" I pointed an accusatory finger at him. "And there is *nothing* wrong with this dress, by the way. It's lovely and perfectly suitable for a formal wedding."

"Perfectly suitable," Zakary repeated. "You

talk all prim, do tequila shots, and wear clothing designed to drive men crazy."

I shook my head. "You're insane."

"You know what?" he said. "You're the one who *makes* me insane." And with that he closed his hands over my upper arms, yanked me to my toes, and kissed me.

CHAPTER NINE

The kiss was unlike any we'd shared before: Passionate, sultry and intense. So very *intense.* When he grabbed my hair and tugged my head back to deepen the kiss, I responded without a moment's hesitation.

My bag hit the floor with a thud, and my heart slammed against my ribs. *Finally!* Was my one clear thought.

After a few moments he lifted his mouth from mine. "Amanda." He searched my eyes. "Did I ever really know you at all?"

"Get to know me." I purred the invitation. "Right now,"

"I think that—"

"That you should shut up and kiss me again," I ordered and plastered my lips to his.

His response had my belly quivering, and my heart racing. He pushed my back against the wall, and his hands began to race all over me. I dropped my fingers to his chest to test the firm muscles beneath that trim tux jacket and shirt.

When he molded a hand to my breast, I slid both of my hands to his waist, yanked his shirt free, and moaned in frustration when he captured my hands in one of his own. I strained against him, desperate to touch him the way I'd always longed to.

Our kiss continued, and it was all open mouths, and tongues with a dangerous edge of teeth. He nipped my bottom lip and I hissed at the pleasurable sting. I returned the favor, and heard his low growl in response.

Gone was the gentle man who'd once courted me so thoughtfully. In my arms was a man trembling on the very edge of control, and I wanted to pull him over the edge with me, and see what happened when he finally let loose.

I felt the coolness of the air on my legs, seconds before his fingers danced past my knees. He had pushed the skirt of my dress up and out of his way, and in answer I hitched a leg up and around his hip, and still our mouths never left each other's. I drew him closer to me, felt the proof of his desire, and then his fingers slid over the knife sheath I had strapped to my upper thigh.

Instantly the kiss stopped. He pulled back and glanced down at the sheath. Still nose-to-nose with each other, we stood there panting. Wrapped around him, I trembled in frustration waiting to see what he would do, and how he would react to the discovery. He searched my face for a long moment. With a shaky exhale he closed his eyes and rested his forehead against mine.

When he lifted his head and at last met my eyes, his entire expression had changed. Deliberately, he reached back and silently unhooked my ankle from behind his back.

I let my leg slide down and as soon as both my feet hit the ground, he stepped away from me completely.

"Why are you wearing a blade?" His voice was low and rough.

It was actually an athame, but he didn't want —or need—to know that. I brushed my skirt down into place, concealing the ritual blade in its sheath. "For the same reason that you carry a gun when you're off duty, Zakary."

"That's completely different!" he snapped.

"No." I shook my head. "Actually it's precisely the same."

"Bullshit!"

I lifted my chin. "The last time you were in this house, you were given a hint of some of the more dangerous things that I can encounter."

He narrowed his eyes. "You're telling me that you expect another freak show to happen tonight? Here, at the wedding?"

I flinched at the words 'freak show'. To make sure my voice was composed, I gave myself a moment.

"Well?" he demanded.

"No, I didn't expect there to be another incident," I said. "However, I believe there is a motto about being prepared?"

"Jesus!" He backed up another step and scrubbed a hand over his face.

"I take it you find this fact disconcerting?"

"That's one way to put it." His angry gaze started at the top of my head and traveled slowly down to my toes. "I swear that I see at least three *different* women when I look at you."

"Three?" I asked, confused.

"You still sound like the smart, classy librarian I fell for. And there's this beautiful, passionate redhead I see in front of me...Wearing a velvet dress with her hair falling down her back." With a sigh, he shook his head. "Finally, I see you as you were the other night. In torn jeans, a black lace camisole and covered in occult tattoos..."

"Zakary—" I reached out for him, trying to make him understand.

He eased away from my outstretched hand. "You called it magick, but the powers you were, wielding—I suppose is the best way to describe it. That's the image I can't get past."

I let my hand drop. "I see."

"I shouldn't have kissed you, or touched you tonight," he said quietly.

"I wanted you to," I said. "If you hadn't found the blade we'd be making love right now."

"It wouldn't have been making love," Zakary

said, bluntly. "It would have been sex. Basically, sex with a stranger, and that's not something I care to do. It's not who *I* am, Amanda."

I had no reply to that. Suddenly cold, I hugged my elbows.

"I need to get back to the wedding," he said.

"As a member of the wedding party, you absolutely should."

"Will you be all right up here, alone?" he started to laugh. "What am I even saying? Of course you will."

"Yes," I said, briskly. "I'll be absolutely fine."

"Goodbye, Amanda." He nodded and walked away, re-tucking his shirt, and straightening his suit as he went.

I felt tears well up and I fought them back. Watching him leave hurt like hell.

There he went, the man of my dreams. Gone from me because I'd kept secrets from him. When he'd found out the truth, he couldn't stomach who I actually was. My knees turned to jello and I didn't trust them to hold my weight anymore.

Don't let him make you cry, I told myself, dropping down to the window seat. My throat ached at the effort it took not to let the tears fall. *Zakary Parker wouldn't break me...*I decided. And my life would go on. What I needed to do was to put on a brave face, go back downstairs, and dance with my best friend at her sister's wedding.

In a couple of minutes. As soon as I could convince my legs to support me.

Right now, I needed to regroup. I pulled my glasses off and pressed my fingers to the bridge of my nose.

I felt the softest of touches on my shoulder, and my breath left me in a rush. I held incredibly still for a moment, forgetting to even breathe as the fragrance of lilacs washed over me. A gentle hand begin to caress my hair, and slowly I turned my head.

I wasn't alone after all, and that discovery had me shoving my glasses back on my face as quickly as I could.

A young woman sat beside me, but she wasn't corporeal. She was a spirit. She wore a yellow day dress in the style of the mid 1800's.

Her hair was dark red, and she held a bouquet of lilacs in her lap.

"Hello," I said, carefully.

"Don't be sad, darling." I heard her words, clear as day.

I'd never encountered such a peaceful spirit. The energy coming from her was practically maternal. "Who are you?" I managed to ask as adrenalin raced through me.

She gave me a shy smile. "Victoria."

"Victoria Midnight? I asked.

In answer she nodded.

"Why are you here?" I asked.

"To watch over you." She reached out and patted my hair again.

"Why are you watching over *me*?"

"Because I'm yours," she said, and disappeared.

I leapt off the window seat. "*I'm yours*?" I repeated. "What's that supposed to mean?"

But there was no answer. I was alone once again, and the window seat was empty except for the clutch of fresh lilac blossoms and green leaves that she'd left behind.

I reached out expecting the flowers to fade

away, and to my shock discovered that they were quite real.

***

Deputy Zakary Parker was the least of my worries now. I took the bouquet directly to Estella. I recalled that she'd once told me she'd dreamt about Victoria and Pierre-Michel having a picnic and that he'd given Victoria lilacs.

"Let me go and get Dru," she said. "Nobody knows more about plants than she does."

While Estella went to locate her sister, I stepped up to the bar and asked for a ginger ale.

Drusilla arrived a moment after my soda did, and together the three of us moved over to a table and sat.

"What can you tell me about these?" I asked, holding out the bouquet.

"What a cute Tussie-mussie!" she said, taking the bouquet for a closer inspection.

Estella gave me a significant look, but I shook my head, wanting to hear Drusilla's thoughts and reactions.

Dru gave the flowers an appreciative sniff.

"Where in the world did you get lilacs at this time of year?"

"I found them upstairs," I said.

Drusilla frowned. "That's odd, Cammy didn't have any lilacs in her wedding flowers."

"I know the flowers are out of season," I said. "But is it possible to get them this time of year, commercially?"

"Sure, if you have an unlimited budget," Drusilla said. "But honestly, lilacs are expensive and *difficult* to use as a cut flower. They wilt very quickly."

Estella flashed her sister a smile. "Thanks, Dru. I figured you would know."

"Happy to help," Drusilla said, and then her attention was caught by something else. "Oh look! They're going to cut the cake!"

Drusilla left to go and watch, while Estella silently studied the bouquet.

"By the old gods." I blew out a long shaky breath, picked up my soda, and drained it.

"What are you thinking?" Estella asked.

I set the glass down with a snap. "I'm thinking that there's *much* more going on than we knew."

"In the language of flowers, purple lilacs symbolize a 'first love'."

"I'm pretty sure that I am *not* Victoria's first love," I said, dryly.

My comment had Estella rolling her eyes. "Yeah, but seriously," she asked, "where were you when she appeared?"

"Third floor, by a window seat." And as soon as I said it out loud it hit me. "The spot where you and Chauncey were——"

"Taken for a ride a few months ago." Estella finished for me.

"I was going to say, *possessed*." I blew out a long breath. "That's the very same place that you saw in your dream. The one with Pierre-Michel and Victoria——"

"Getting it on."

"Please stop finishing my sentences." I frowned at her. "It's——"

"Annoying?" Estella grinned.

I rubbed my forehead, where a headache was starting to brew. "I was so distracted by the deputy that it didn't even dawn on me the importance of and history of the location." *That was foolish,* I thought. *Clearly I wasn't at my best when the deputy was around.*

Estella nudged me with an elbow to get my attention. "So were you and the deputy up there putting the window seat to use again?"

"Ah, no." I said.

"Here I was figuring you two were gonna go at it. There's some serious chemistry there."

I dropped my head to my hands with a groan.

"I'm just saying," Estella went on. "I was sort of disappointed when you came back downstairs so quickly, and separately."

I lifted my head and glared at her.

She patted my shoulder. "Did you two have another argument? What's he pissed off about this time?"

"Basically it was a replay of our last disagreement," I said, not wanting to get into all the details.

"I'm sorry," she said contritely.

Chauncey Marquette approached our table. "It's two of my favorite ladies," he said and suavely set a glass of wine in front of me, and a beer in a frosted mug front of Estella. "Mind if I join you?"

"Have a seat." I gestured toward a chair.

"Victoria's ghost paid Amanda a visit while she was upstairs, a bit ago." Estella said, without preamble.

Chauncey's shoulder's stiffened. "Are you all right?" he asked me.

Estella leaned forward. "She left—"

I cut off Estella's words by clamping my hand on her knee. "She's left the building," I lied smoothly. "Everything is fine."

Chauncey shook his head. "I think this place really is spook central."

Estella chuckled. "That's exactly what Camilla calls it."

I was desperate to have a few moments of peace where I could think about my encounter with the spirit of Victoria Midnight, but it seemed that Estella was going to stick to me like glue. Even worse, now Chauncey apparently felt he needed to stay as well.

The music switched to a slow song and I saw my opportunity. "Why don't you two go and dance? That's a great song."

Beside me I felt Estella stiffen in her chair. "Oh that's okay." Her airy voice contradicted her nervous reaction. "I'm sure Marquette would rather sit this one out. He's got a bum leg, you know."

Offended, he raised his brow. "Have you danced tonight, Estella?"

"Yes," she said, sipping her beer. "I danced when the wedding party was called out to the floor."

Chauncey stood up and held out his hand. "Dance with me, Estella."

From my vantage point I saw Estella gulp nervously. "Nah, I'm good," she said setting her beer down.

"What's the matter, Flores?" Chauncey asked. "Are you afraid you'll step on my toes again?"

"I've *never* stepped on your toes!" Estella scowled at him.

"Well then?" His tone of voice made it basically a dare, and I knew my friend wouldn't back down from that.

"*Por el amor de dios!*" Estella stood up. "Fine, fine. Let's go dance."

It made me smile to watch her grab his hand and haul him off to the dance floor. Now that I was alone, I pulled my phone out and took a few pictures of the nosegay Victoria had left. Afterwards, I hit the notes app and typed in everything that she'd said. I noted the date, time and location of the manifestation, the flowers in the bouquet, and Victoria's appearance. I slipped my phone back in my purse, sat back, and sipped my wine. Telling myself to settle down and to think analytically.

I would need to talk to Estella and find out everything she knew about Victoria Midnight. Maybe get a look at her journal where she wrote her prophecies...this was an important encounter, and there was something I was missing...

The music changed and Sia's, *Cheap Thrills,* came on. I was yanked from my thoughts at the sight of Estella, who was boogying her way back to the table. She had Brooke with her and from the grins on their faces, they were up to no good.

"Hi!" Brooke said and grabbed ahold of one of my elbows. "Estella said you needed cheering up. Let's dance."

"Oh, I don't think that's a good idea," I tried to say.

"Ha!" Estella tossed her head. "You gonna let a man keep you sitting over in the corner by yourself?"

Well, when she put it that way. "Screw it." I decided and stood up to kick off my heels. "Let's get warmed up for that table-top dancing later."

"Atta girl," Estella cheered.

I ended up on the dance floor with Estella, her sisters, and Brooke. Even the bride was grooving. After three fast songs, I saw Estella go and make a request to the DJ. I burst out laughing when the song from the new Ghostbusters movie began to play.

"I figured it was appropriate for us," Estella shouted over *Good Girls,* by Elle King.

"I do what the good girls should never do," I agreed with a laugh, and danced along to the music that was banging out of the speakers.

***

There'd been no dancing on tables, but I had drank more at the wedding reception than I typically did. Estella drove me home with my car and returned it to me Sunday afternoon. I found it intensely annoying that she suffered no ill effects from the party. She made some cheerful comment about being a bartender, and I supposed that holding her liquor well was practically a job requirement. Still, I hadn't had a hangover in years, and it was hideous.

I spent the day cleaning, puttering around my house, and listening to holiday music on the radio. I lit cinnamon scented candles for healing and protection, and combined with the woody pine aroma from the live tree, the house smelled like Yuletide. By the evening I felt practically back to normal, so I baked a batch of holiday cookies and wrapped a few gifts, sliding the presents under the tree in my living room. To my surprise, the spray of lilacs from Victoria was still holding. I'd tucked it in a vase of water after the wedding and they were scenting my kitchen nicely.

When I opened the library on Monday, the Midnight—Ames wedding was the talk of the village. I had several patrons wanting to chat me up about it. Besides the typical demand for holiday decorating and Christmas books, there was also a run on alternative bridal fashion books. I had half expected it. After all, I knew the rhythm of the village as well as anyone. The weather shifted and we got our first snowfall. It was only a dusting, but it was very pretty and it made everything feel more festive.

Estella dropped by Tuesday with an early holiday gift. It was a DNA kit, the sort designed to help you track your family tree. She was so animated and excited over the idea that it was contagious. She had purchased a kit for herself too, and we sat down together, and set up our profiles online. We laughed for a half hour over having to spit in the provided container to collect the DNA samples, and the next morning I dropped by the post office and mailed out our kits.

I knew she had done that to try and give me an opening to tell the Midnights about my being a fourth cousin. It wasn't a bad way to break the ice, I supposed. The kits took four to six weeks for the results to come in, and after everything, maybe revealing this secret would help me get over what I'd lost from keeping so many others.

Later in the afternoon I was re-shelving

books when I was ambushed. My assailant came in low, and the books I'd been holding went flying as I fought to stay on my feet.

"Hi, 'Manda!" The voice of my attacker belonged to one of my favorite patrons. Four-year-old Mark Ellison. With a grin, he gave my legs a hug.

"Hello, Mark," I patted his back, very pleased to see him doing so well. "What sort of books are you looking for today?"

"Books about planes!"

"Mark," the voice belonged to his father. "You can't tackle the librarian every time you see her."

"She's my friend," Mark said, still hanging on to me.

I picked the child up and set him on my hip. "I'll always be your friend." I smiled to the father. "Hello, Mr. Ellison,"

"Sorry about this," he began to apologize.

"Not to worry," I assured him. "I'm happy to see you both doing so well."

"Can you help me find more books?" Mark flashed a smile and I saw he was missing a tooth.

"Hey, you lost a tooth!" I said. "That's exciting."

The blonde boy bounced on my hip. "The tooth fairy gave me a dollar!"

"Wow. Really?" I did my best to sound impressed by the news. "I tell you what..." I said. "Let's me, you, and your daddy go see what else we can find for you about airplanes."

"Thank you, Miss Beaumont," his father said.

"I'm here to help." I smiled and the three of us went to the children's section together.

After the Ellisons left, I went back to my shelving. I rolled the half-empty cart down a row and stopped at the appropriate section, but before I could put the first book away, my stomach dropped and a premonition hit me like a freight train.

CHAPTER TEN

Something was wrong. Something had happened. Panic washed over me and I tried to breathe my way through it. I hated it when these happened. The gut feeling that something was *wrong,* but with no real information. I pressed a hand to my stomach, and mentally ran down the list of my nearest and dearest hoping for a 'hit' or confirmation to the warning I'd received. But it was difficult to put a pin in it.

The premonition had to do with family, I was sure of that. But I wasn't sure exactly where or who. I reached for the cell phone in my blazer pocket. I'd call my parents first and check on them, make sure they were all right in Florida.

Before I could call, I saw Zakary walk in the doors of the library. His face was serious and his mouth unsmiling. He scanned the library, spotted me, and strode directly over.

I put the phone back in my pocket. "Deputy?" I coolly inclined my head. "What brings you to the library today?"

"Amanda," he said without smiling. "There's been a break-in at your house."

I blinked. "That's not possible."

"Your neighbor, Mrs. Prideaux, called to report a disturbance. I arrived on the scene and found your doors open and the inside of your house ransacked."

"A disturbance?" I could only repeat what he'd said, and stand there while my mind tried to make sense of what I was hearing. *But there are powerful wards guarding the house,* my mind argued. *The magickal protection had been built up over generations of Beaumonts...That simply wasn't possible.*

"The Sherriff is there now securing the scene." He took me by the elbow and steered me along. "Let's go get your things."

"Amanda?" Jenna's worried voice called from across the library floor. "What's happened?"

"Jenna, could you hold down the fort?" I asked, ducking into my office and grabbing my coat. "I've been informed that someone broke into my house."

She pressed her hand to her chest in shock. "Of course! You go! Let me know if I can help in any way."

"We need to go," Zakary said. "Right now."

"This can't be happening," I said, shrugging my coat on.

"It's not uncommon for robberies to occur before Christmas," Zakary said.

"You don't understand, Deputy. I have an advanced sort of security system," I said, trying to wrap my mind around his words. "No living person could break *in* to my home..."

My words trailed off as a horrible possibility hit me.

What if no one had broken in. I thought. *What if something had broken out instead.*

My god, the painting of Pierre-Michel. It had been locked up and magickally confined in my cellar for the past few weeks...

Had his spirit somehow broken free?

***

I tried to remain calm as we drove across the village. But my heart was pounding and my palms were sweating. *How could my containment spells have failed? Another practitioner perhaps? Could there have been an all out magickal attack on the property? Who would even have the firepower to accomplish such a thing?*

Zakary's voice cut into my thoughts. "Did you have anything of particular value stored in the house? Jewelry, or expensive electronics?"

"No." I tried to speak calmly and to maintain my composure. "Nothing like that."

"Have you noticed anything suspicious lately?" he asked.

As compared to what? I wondered. *Like the ghosts I saw roaming the streets last week, or the rumors of some sort of monster harassing joggers along the river road? Would that be classified as 'suspicious' to you, Zakary?*

I turned my face away from his and stared out the passenger window while my mind continued to race. In addition to the portrait, all of Louisa's journals and spell books were stored in the cellar in a locked safe. Even though I'd recently reinforced the charms and added more protection spells to guard the cellar, what if the wards had completely failed?

My gods, that sort of magickal information in the wrong hands would be catastrophic. That particular thought had a bead of sweat running down my back despite the cold temperatures and the snow on the ground.

"Amanda, are you sure you locked the house when you left this morning?"

There was no point in explaining to the deputy that I never did something as simple as putting a key in a door. Besides, chances were he wouldn't respond very well to the truth...Hadn't his behavior over the past couple of weeks demonstrated that clearly enough?

He'd barely put the cruiser in park before I was opening the car door. I stood and saw for myself that my front door was currently hanging crookedly from its hinges. Even while I hesitated over the discovery, my mind was working, and dissecting the scene. The wooden frame was broken. The door itself swung back and forth, creaking in the wind.

As if the door had exploded out—and not been kicked or forced in.

Ignoring the deputy's order to wait, I rushed around to the deck, went right into my kitchen, and broken glass crunched beneath my boots. "By the old gods," I whispered. The room was in shambles. Cabinet doors were broken, dishes and glasses had been smashed, and my vintage green glass canisters of sugar and flour appeared to have imploded. Their contents had been thrown everywhere.

The distinctive smell of sulfur assailed my senses, and that meant only one thing, *evil*. Shocked to discover that sort of energy in my home, I gasped, stepping instinctively backwards.

"Amanda." Zakary said, as I bumped solidly into him. "Be careful, you could get hurt."

I pulled away and noticed movement from across the room. My godfather, Sherriff Randall, was standing in the doorway to the dining room. "I'm sorry, Mandy," he said, holding his arms open for me. "They made a hell of a mess."

I walked through broken glass and straight into the man's arms. "I'm glad you're here." I said, ignoring the deputy.

"I'll help you with this, honey." The Sherriff gave me a bear hug. "First I need you to walk through the house with me so we can check to see if anything is missing."

"Okay," I managed, even though it was muffled against his shoulder.

"Would you like me to call your folks?" he asked.

"No. Not for this. Let them enjoy their retirement."

"I understand." He nodded. "Is there anything else you need?"

"Have you or any of the deputies seen my cat?"

"No, we haven't." He patted my back. "Maybe she'd hiding. Animals do that sometimes."

"I could look for her," Zakary volunteered. "What does she look like?"

"She's a long haired, black cat," I said, turning to face him. "She has an ID tag and an orange collar—"

He chuckled. "Of course, you have a black cat."

I stiffened at his derision, but before I could reply, Sherriff Randall dismissed him. "Deputy, you may leave. Your services are no longer required at this scene."

"I'm sorry, Amanda," Zakary said. "That came out wrong."

The Sherriff glared. "I gave you an order, Deputy."

With no choice, Zakary silently left.

My godfather squeezed my shoulders sympathetically and took me through the house. It was hard to look at the damage that had been done. The decorated tree was knocked over. The presents I'd so carefully wrapped were trashed. The paper shredded and the contents were dumped.

Discarded on the floor, yet not taken. My brain clicked that information away as we toured the damage. My bedroom was as bad as the downstairs had been. The bed had been stripped, the mattress knocked off the frame. My clothes had been thrown around, and dresser drawers hung open with their contents spilling out. Both the antique mirror above my chest of drawers and the one attached to my old vanity table were smashed. All of the perfume and makeup bottles had been knocked off and were scattered, broken over the floor.

While the Sherriff's department photographed the mess and checked for a point of entry, I surveyed the damage and made a mental list of things that were destroyed. But while many of my possessions were broken, smashed or ruined, nothing was stolen.

"I need to check the cellar," I said, giving the man a significant look.

"Your father's old workshop?" he asked quietly.

"Yes."

While my godfather knew the cellar as my father's workshop, he was still unaware of the complete catalogue of magickal items that it held. The Sherriff cleared his throat. "We can check together."

"Thank you," I said.

Oddly, the cellar had suffered no damage at all. Which made me very uneasy. I immediately checked the room that was holding the portrait of Pierre-Michel, and found the entrance to the chamber to be untouched. However, I still wanted eyes on that crated portrait.

Once I opened the chamber, I was relieved to see that nothing had been disturbed. The extra magick I'd piled on to that room after storing the portrait seemed to be holding. The lead-lined safe that held Louisa's journals and spell books was also intact. The magickal tools and the personal journals from all the past Guardians were still inside of their cabinet, and were as neat as I'd left them...which should have made me feel better.

But it did not.

If the damage hadn't been caused by the spirit of Pierre-Michel, then what had torn apart the house? I wondered.

"How odd," I said out loud. "That the cellar was untouched."

"I suppose the intruders didn't have time to get to the cellar," The Sherriff said.

"I suppose not," I said—strictly for his benefit. It made no sense that the cellar with all of its spell books and magickal tools, weapons, and trinkets had been left alone. In fact, the more I looked around, the more I was sure that no living person had broken in.

"Either that, or they came down the steps, got spooked and ran." The Sherriff grinned.

Once we were back on the main floor, the Sherriff went to temporarily secure the front door for me. I stood in my living room surveying the chaos and realized in addition to the clean-up, I would also have to perform an extensive magickal *cleansing* on the house. The proof was right there in front of me.

The scent of sulfur lingered on the air, and my trio of blooming orchids had withered dramatically. The large palm, potted dracaena, pothos, and the lucky bamboo in my living room had all turned brown. The pretty moth orchid that had been a centerpiece of the dining room table was also dead. I touched a leaf and it crumbled to dust in my hand.

Whatever had done this was so thoroughly evil that my familiar had run away, and all the plants in the house had perished from the exposure to its negative energy.

The house felt empty and lifeless, as if the magickal spirit of the home had been snuffed out. For me, that was the biggest loss of all.

I felt slightly detached from the chaos that was around me, and maybe that was shock. I somehow still managed to hold my emotions in check, until I discovered that not only had the holiday décor been ripped from the mantle, but a cherished framed photo had been knocked off as well.

"Oh, no." I bent over to pick it up and found that the glass was shattered, and the photo damaged. It was a picture of me and my parents from the last time I'd visited them in Florida. The three of us were standing arm in arm on the beach at sunset, all mugging for the camera while my mother took a selfie.

It was one of those silly photos that perfectly captures a moment, and to see it damaged, had my eyes welling with tears.

This destruction was petty and spiteful, and designed to hurt me. This was a retaliation or punishment of sorts. I wiped my eyes and set the photo back carefully on the mantle. When a member of the Sherriff's department popped in to inform me they'd be leaving soon, I nodded and picked my way over the debris, and headed back toward the kitchen.

I stopped short when I saw Estella standing in the remains of my kitchen. "Damn, girlfriend," she said, looking around. "You sure know how to party."

"There's been a little excitement," I said.

"What in the holy hell happened in here?" she asked.

"I'm not sure," I said, as the last members of the team passed through the kitchen on their way out. "I was working at the library, and the Sherriff's department came and got me. They are ruling this a break-in."

Before I could say anything else Sherriff Randall strolled in from the living room. "I used some boards from the garage and nailed the front door shut for you, Mandy." He set a hammer and a box of nails down on the counter. "You will probably want to do the same to the backdoor before you leave."

"I'm not leaving my home," I told him. "I can secure it for tonight. I'll make some calls and get a repairman out here in the morning."

"You shouldn't stay here alone," he argued.

"She won't be alone," Estella announced.

"I'll stay here with her."

After a few moments of me assuring my godfather that I'd be fine, I finally got him to leave. Estella and I watched out the kitchen windows until all the Sherriff's cars left. Once they were gone, I blew out a long sigh of relief.

"This wasn't a break in," Estella said. "The doors weren't kicked in."

"Yes, I know. The doors were both blown *out*," I said, softly.

"God it stinks in here!" Estella waved a hand in front of her face. "What *is* that smell?"

"Sulfur."

"Are you freaking kidding me?"

"No. I am quite serious." I blew out a long breath. "This wasn't a mundane break in, Estella. This attack was something else entirely."

"It toasted the house plants, but didn't touch the stained glass pentacle in the window above the sink." Estella pointed out.

"No," I said, looking for myself, "it didn't." The glass was still shining bright, while all the plants on the windowsill below were quite dead.

I stood there, considering the damage to the kitchen and wondered where to begin. The old seeded glass in the upper cabinets on either side of the window were shattered, and the magickal cabinets in the laundry room had been...I suppose the best word was, *obliterated*. As if she'd clued into my thoughts, Estella walked over to check the laundry room.

"Oh, your spell casting supplies! Everything is smashed and broken."

I took my glasses off and rubbed my eyes. "Yes, I know."

"What could make tumbled stones crack like this?" she asked as she rooted through what was left of years of carefully cultivated goods. "Holy shit, your boxes of spell candles...they're all melted. The incense and candle holders are smashed, and your herbs, and powdered incense...it's like it got flung everywhere!"

"It's all destroyed." With a sigh, I slipped my glasses back on and squared my shoulders.

"What could do something like that?" She asked with very large eyes. "What the hell did you piss off?"

"I'm not sure yet. But whatever it was, it was

already *inside* the house."

"An inside job?" Estella stood with her hands on her hips. "I wonder how it got in?

"I'm not sure," I repeated. *I'd rarely run across a practitioner with enough firepower to have pulled this off...*I thought to myself. *So who or what had done it?*

Estella pulled her phone from her back pocket. "I'm going to call out the troops and then we can get started putting this place back together."

I tried to wave her off. "That's not necessary."

"Bullshit. You're family, and if I've learned anything since I moved to Ames Crossing its that the Midnights rally together when there's any sort of crisis." Estella tapped on her phone screen. "Gabriella?" she said. "Hey, it's Estella. There's been a break-in at Amanda's house. They trashed the place, and we could use some help over here."

I stopped myself from arguing further, grabbed my kitchen broom, and swept the broken glass to one side of the kitchen floor. Hopefully, that would stop any more broken glass from being tracked through the house while Estella made her calls.

Clearly I would need to put on something sturdier than the dress slacks and blazer I'd worn to work. I went to my room and changed into a pair of jeans and an old sweater.

Estella came up and helped me refold all my clothes, remake the bed, and put what could be salvaged from my personal things away. I found my tennis shoes, and while we searched the house for Nyx, Estella and I opened every damned window to air the place out.

"Nyx is smart," Estella said patting my shoulder. "She probably hit the road when the doors blew open. Once it's safe, she'll come back."

Within an hour of Estella making her phone calls, the daughters of Midnight, and their men, descended in force on my home. The matriarch, Priscilla, arrived first with a bucket of cleaning supplies, and old willow broom, *and* a picnic basket of food. Drusilla, Garrett Rivers, and Brooke James arrived next. They volunteered to work on the living and dining room for me.

"I brought a few of those construction-grade

trash bags along," Drusilla said, handing them over. "Thought they might come in handy for the broken glass."

"I can fix your Christmas tree!" Brooke volunteered. "Dru says I have a good eye for decorating."

"Thank you, Brooke," I said, while everyone dove right in.

Gabriella and Philippe arrived next, and to my shock, even Chauncey Marquette showed up ready to work. "It's the least I could do," he said with a smile.

I smiled back. "Thank you, Chauncey."

Gabriella unbuttoned her coat, wrinkling her nose at the smell. "Ick, sulfur. There's some awfully negative energy still lingering inside your home."

"Yes, I agree." I reached to take her coat and found myself enveloped in a big hug instead. "Thank you for coming," I said, my throat going tight with emotions.

"What are friends for?" She released me and flashed a big smile. "Don't you worry. I had Philippe bring some tools and I brought some magickal goodies along too. We'll do a cleansing after we get things put back together."

"That was very smart," I managed to say.

"That's me," she hooked a thumb toward the big canvas bag she had over her shoulder. "I am very smart, just ask Philippe."

"You are a creative genius, *ma belle*," he said dryly, holding a five-gallon bucket full of tools.

"Where's Danielle?" I asked the couple.

Philippe set the bucket on the kitchen floor. "She's with Nicole and Max."

"If Cammy wasn't on her honeymoon, you know she'd have been here too," Gabriella said.

I smiled. "Well, nevertheless, I appreciate your help."

"You helped us when no one else could," Philippe rested a hand on my shoulder. "My family and I are glad to be able to return the favor."

"You are so very suave, Philippe," Estella said.

Chauncey raised his eyebrows at her comment. "You will find that *all* the Marquette men are."

"Are what?" Estella asked him with a sneer. "Arrogant?"

Before Chauncey could reply, Priscilla stepped neatly between them. "We should begin working on the mess in the kitchen," she said. "Chauncey, you can start by removing the broken glass from the cabinet doors, and I'll see what I can salvage in here. Estella, you should work on the laundry area."

"Thank you, Mrs. Midnight," I managed to say. The older woman made me a tad nervous. There was something about her. She was powerful. You could tell in the way she carried herself, *and* she was adored. That was obvious by the way her family treated her.

Everyone set to work. Estella tackled the laundry room cabinets, while Chauncey worked on the cabinet doors. He was surprisingly handy for a retired race car driver. He and Estella kept ragging on each other as they worked on opposite sides of the room. It was almost entertaining enough to make me smile.

A while later, Brooke drug a huge trash bag into the kitchen. "A bunch of your ornaments and holiday stuff were broken. But I saved what I could."

"Thank you," I said.

She smiled. "Garrett said I should put this bag out on the back deck?"

I helped her pick it up and together we hauled it outside. The sun was starting to set and I lifted my head toward the cold breeze, allowing the wind to rid me of any lingering negativity. Shutting my eyes, I stood still for a moment and tried to center myself.

"Dru is working on the orchids for you...cutting them back—or something." Brooke's voice had me opening my eyes. "She thinks the orchids will be okay."

"Well, she'd know," I said. "I've never met a more talented gardener."

Brooke walked over to stand next to me. For a moment we silently watched the sun set. "Cammy taught me that the element of air can cleanse your aura." Brooke piped up.

I smiled at the girl. "She did, did she?"

"Uh huh," Brooke nodded, tucking a strand of ginger hair behind her ear. "That's the reason all windows are open in the house, and that's what you were doing, right? You're letting the wind blow away the bad vibes."

I blew out a long breath. "That would be

correct on all counts."

Brooke checked carefully over her shoulder before she spoke. "You sure do have a lot of magickal stuff in your house. Like, books and things."

Estella had helped me to try and secure the most overtly magickal objects and books *before* her family had arrived. I suppose we'd missed a few items. I smiled down at the girl.

"I wasn't snooping, Miss Beaumont!" She was quick to assure me. "I just notice things."

"You're very observant. That's a good trait in a magician."

"I'm not a magician yet." Brooke smiled shyly. "I'm still learning. Dru and Cammy have been teaching me things. Gran, she makes me and Estella memorize all these rules and stuff."

"Rules create order out of chaos," I told her, and was pleased at the thought of the elegant Priscilla Midnight taking both Estella and this young girl under her wing.

"I wondered about you, those times I came to the library to research goddesses, history, and stuff," Brooke said. "You never even reacted when I asked for help looking for books."

"Please call me Amanda," I said. "I enjoyed helping you with the search into your ancestry. On Thanksgiving when I saw the heraldry of Melusine above your fireplace it all fell into place."

"Most people don't get that," she said, "the magick stuff."

I gave the girl a friendly elbow nudge. "But we're not most people, are we?"

CHAPTER ELEVEN

With all the extra hands the house was coming back together quickly. It still felt empty, even with all the people standing around and eating off paper plates in my kitchen. It made me wonder if, not unlike a psychic injury, the magick within the house would need time and care to recover from whatever spiritual damage it had sustained.

"Thank you, Mrs. Midnight, for thinking to bring along food," I said, while everyone dug into sandwiches and potato salad. "It was very kind of you."

"You're welcome, Amanda." Priscilla sat at the kitchen table and dabbed her lips with a paper towel.

"Thank you everyone, for helping me put the

house back in order." I reached in the fridge to pass Brooke, and then Estella, a bottle of water. "I appreciate it more than you know."

"Nonsense." Priscilla waved my thank you away. "It's what family does."

The second bottle of water dropped from my fingers and bounced off the freshly scrubbed kitchen floor. I gaped at the woman in shock. "I'm sorry?"

She gave me a serene sort of smile. "Family, however distant, is still family, my dear."

I shot a look at Estella. *Had she revealed one of my secrets after all?*

Estella held up her hands. "I didn't say anything. I swear!"

"Gran?" Drusilla set her plate on the counter. "What are you talking about."

"The Beaumonts are cousins to the Midnights, didn't you know?" Priscilla said.

"No," Drusilla said. "I didn't know that."

"After your grandfather passed, I spent years researching the Midnight family tree. As I am the only magickal practitioner from the Curtis family—"

"Curtis?" Estella asked.

"Curtis is my maiden name" she explained. "I found the Midnight's magickal lineage quite fascinating. Over the years it's become a passion. I do consider myself a bit of a genealogy buff."

Gabriella shifted her eyes from her grandmother to me. "So are you saying that Amanda is related to us?"

"I am," I said.

The reaction to my announcement had jaws dropping, all except for Estella. She simply folded her arms over her chest and grinned at everyone.

"Technically, we're fourth cousins," I said to the people gathered in the room. "Tobias Midnight was one of four Midnight children, and he was *your* direct ancestor." I motioned to Gabriella, Drusilla, and Estella.

"He was in fact, your four times great grandfather, girls," Priscilla supplied the information. "Tobias also had three younger sisters."

"That's right. I remember, now," Drusilla said. "We'd originally thought that the "Four Stars of Midnight" prophecy was about Tobias and his three sisters."

"But it ended up being about me." Estella retrieved the water bottle I'd dropped from the floor. "I was the fourth daughter of Midnight— the star that had to journey home."

"Right," Gabriella nodded. "Do we know what happened to Tobias' three sisters?"

Priscilla cleared her throat. "From what I found, I know that the eldest of the three, Jenna Midnight, married a merchant and moved to St. Louis."

"That would be correct." I nodded to Priscilla. "While the middle sister, Louisa, married and remained in the village."

"And what about the youngest sister?" Gabriella asked.

"That would have been *Victoria*," Estella reminded them. "The daughter of Midnight from the big scandal of 1847? She was the Seer and wrote all the whacked out poetry—"

"Prophecies," Priscilla corrected.

"Whatever." Estella shrugged. "Victoria was the one who was in love with Pierre-Michel. You know, the love-sick ghosts that possessed me and Chauncey?"

"Despite the love-sick ghosts," I said holding up a hand. "As to the genealogy and how we are connected—*I* am a direct descendant of Louisa Midnight and Eugene Beaumont."

"Another daughter of Midnight," Drusilla said with a slow smile. "That does explain a few of the things that I've seen in your home."

"And it accounts for your expertise on the paranormal," Philippe said, thoughtfully.

Gabriella tilted her head to one side as she studied me. "So have you always known about the family connection, Amanda?"

"Yes," I said.

"Why didn't you tell me, that day I came to you for help with the haunting?" She wanted to know. "Why did you feel you had to keep your heritage a secret?"

"Because it's what the Beaumonts have done for generations."

Drusilla frowned. "Why on earth would they do that?"

"I've heard stories about a widow Beaumont," Brooke broke into the conversation. "We had to do a history report about Ames Crossing. The kids in school all talked about this old lady from the 1800's who lived in the village, and how she cursed the vineyards and anyone who got in her way."

I nodded my head. "That would be my ancestor, Louisa Beaumont."

"Tall tales, sweetheart." Priscilla tried to reassure Brooke. "Idle gossip. Nothing more."

"In this case," I said, "the rumors were quite true." I cleared my throat wanting to be as candid as possible. "One of the reasons the Beaumonts hid their links to the Midnight family line was to appease Tobias and his children. Tobias Midnight didn't want the taint of Louisa's black magick to be associated with his wise craft."

"Fascinating." Priscilla leaned forward in her chair, looking directly at me. "What else do you know about that, Amanda?"

"I know that Victor Beaumont, Louisa's only child, struck an agreement with his Uncle Tobias. In which the Beaumonts would sever all ties with the Midnight family."

"Whoa," Gabriella said. "That's harsh."

I nodded to her. "But necessary. Since that time the Beaumonts have hidden their links to the Midnight family... At least we had. Until today."

"Hmmm..." Drusilla stared like she'd never seen me before. "I see."

"Don't be mad at her, Dru," Estella said. "Amanda had damn good reasons for keeping this all a secret."

"The Midnights have had their share of secrets too over the years," Gabriella said, resting her hand on Dru's shoulder. "As for me, I'm not angry. I'm simply surprised."

Drusilla started to chuckle. "Well, Cammy is going to be thrilled to hear about all of this. I can't imagine how many more sticky notes she's going to put on that journal of Victoria's."

"Speaking of which," I said. "I'd like to examine that journal for myself."

"Of course. We'll arrange for that." Priscilla nodded. "However, we still have work to do. The house needs to be cleansed and all the negative energy from the attack removed."

"Can I help?" Brooke wanted to know, looking from Priscilla to me.

"How are you at holding a cardinal point in a ritual circle?" I asked the twelve-year-old.

She bounced up and down. "I can do it!"

"Put her in the western quarter," Drusilla suggested. "She has an affinity for the element of water."

"Wait until you guys see Amanda when she's doing magick," Estella said with a smile. "She's a total bad-ass."

"I'll bet she is." Gabriella smiled and rubbed her hands together. "Let's get started."

***

I'd never worked magick with anyone other than my father before. It was very different casting a cleansing spell upon the house with five other women. Plus, I had no idea if my type of magick would be compatible to the wise-women techniques and herbal craft the daughters of Midnight performed.

Drusilla had taken the north and invoked the element of earth. Gabriella stood in the eastern quarter and summoned the element of air. Estella held the southern point and had called in the element of fire, while Brooke finished up the four quarters by inviting the element of water in from the west.

I kept the ritual straightforward. Not only was our magick compatible, the energy we raised was powerful. The lights in the house began to pulse, and as we finished up, the foul odor was banished completely. The house again smelled like pine and cinnamon, and it gave me hope that the magick of the home wasn't lost forever.

Once everyone had gone home, I walked around and took in the changes to my home. I made a list of things I'd need to replace, and another list of items needing to be repaired. As of tonight, most of my secrets had been revealed. The Midnights knew we were fourth cousins, Estella and Gabriella knew about my role as a Guardian, and the deputy...well he knew, and he hadn't been able to accept it.

I set down the notepad I'd been using to make a repair list and decided from this moment on to be frank and candid in *any* conversation I had with my relatives.

And if I ever spoke to the deputy again, I'd do the same. I couldn't go back and change things, but I *could* learn from the mistakes I'd made and go forward.

To please myself, I made some slight changes to the Yule tree. About half of my blue and silver ornaments were gone. In fact, most of my glass ornaments hadn't survived the tree getting knocked over, but Brooke had done a good job putting it back together.

I'd run into Alton, hit a craft store, and see if I could get more to replace them, I decided.

"Let's build a fire and brighten this place up," I said simply to hear my own voice. Once I had the flames snapping, I sat on my couch to watch it. I felt the loss of Nyx's presence keenly. If she were here, she'd have been in her favorite spot basking on the hearth. I hoped that wherever she was tonight, that she was safe and warm.

Pulling my hair down from the ponytail I'd had it in, I rubbed at my scalp. I was plotting how best to cast a spell to call my familiar home, when there was a knock on my door.

I rose to my feet with a sigh, figuring Estella had decided to ignore my request that I be left alone tonight. I walked into the kitchen, saw the visitor through the window, and discovered that the deputy was on my deck. He stood staring back at me through the window, bundled in a heavy coat and scarf against the cold.

Tired, and at the end of my emotional rope, I yanked the door open. "You've got some nerve, showing up to my house after—"

"I believe you've been looking for this?" he interrupted.

I suddenly noticed that he was holding something in his arms. It was Nyx, wrapped in a towel.

The cat's scruffy head popped over Zakary's arm. "Meow?" she cried softly.

"Nyx!" I cried, reaching for my cat.

"Here you go." Zakary handed her over.

"Where did you find her?" I asked, starting to cry.

"I didn't," he said, following me inside and shutting the door. "It was more like she found me."

"How do you mean?"

"She was sitting on the front porch of my house, shivering in the snow, and yowling her head off," he said,

"She went to your house?" I hugged the cat

close. "But that's a couple miles away!"

"I heard the caterwauling, peeked out the front door, and saw her. She came right to me and started pawing at my leg."

Nyx began to purr and burrowed closer to me for comfort. "Who's a smart kitty?" I said to the cat.

"I see you've been busy cleaning up." He glanced around. "Wow, it even smells better in here. How did you get all this accomplished so quickly?"

"Estella and her family came over and helped me."

"That was kind of them," Zakary said. "It *feels* better in the house than it did before. Why is that?"

"Because the daughters of Midnight and I did a cleansing ritual after we straightened up, and scrubbed everything." I spoke plainly, and let the chips fall where they may.

"I see," he said after a moment.

"*Do you?*" I asked, pointedly.

He nodded. "Everyone knows about the Midnights. I'm simply wondering why they would... do all of this?"

"Because that's what family does."

He did a double take. "Are you telling me that you're related to the Midnights?"

I met his gaze and held it. "Yes, Zakary. That is *exactly* what I'm telling you."

"I never knew that—"

"And with the exception of Estella, neither did they. Until tonight."

"More secrets, Amanda?"

"It would be safe to say, that I have considerably less secrets now."

He gave me a long look. "Is this connected to what you told me that night at the mansion? You said your *calling* had been kept a secret for generations."

"That would be correct. I'm surprised you remember what I told you."

"Trust me, it's sort of burned in my mind. It took me a couple weeks to work my way through...everything."

"Well, how lovely for you." I tried, and failed to keep the bite out of my words.

"Can we sit down?" he asked, gently. "I think it's way past time you and I talked, calmly."

I would have to come to some sort of an

understanding with the deputy, I realized. I supposed now was a good a time as ever. Nyx squirmed wanting to get down, so I gently placed her on the floor and unwrapped the towel. She flipped her tail high, trotted directly to her food bowl, and dug in.

We went to the living room. I chose the far end of the couch and sat. Zakary unzipped his coat, set it on a chair, and took the opposite end of the couch. For a few moments we stared at each other. Finally I couldn't take it anymore. "You said you wanted to talk. So talk."

"The day after the incident up at the mansion, Sherriff Randall pulled me into his office and explained a few things to me."

I nodded for him to continue.

"Between that and our conversation, I started to put things together. After the Sherriff had his say, he gave me a key to a locked cabinet in his office. He called it—"

"The Weird Files." I finished the sentence for him.

"I've spent the last few weeks working my way through those files. Some of the papers went back to the mid 1800's. I discovered that your father wasn't the only Hunter, so were your grandfather and great-grandfather."

"Technically we are called *Guardians*," I said. "And it started with Victor Beaumont Jr." I got up to add another log to the fire.

"I didn't see any mentions of other women in the position," Zakary said.

I tossed the log in, and straightened. "That's because I am the first."

"You are? That's sort of cool."

Now it was my turn to do a double take. "This is quite the change in attitude from the other night."

"Well, like I said I've been studying those files, and was trying to wrap my mind around it all. It's fascinating. Then I came across the case of the Ellison boy from last year."

I nodded, instead of replying.

"That case had been a particularly tough one," he said. "Mark Ellison had been only three-years-old at the time of his abduction. We pegged the mother right away as the kidnapper, since the boy's parents had been going through a nasty divorce and the father had sued for full custody."

"Yes, I remember," I said quietly, replacing the fireplace screen.

"Mr. Ellison had claimed that the mother was unstable and abusive. The father had been granted temporary custody, and divorce proceedings had been underway...and *poof*, the child and his mother disappeared."

Nyx trotted into the room and took her favored place on the hearth. I patted her head while Zakary continued to speak.

"I coordinated the search teams looking for that child," Zakary said. "After two weeks we'd begun to give up hope and had started using cadaver dogs...And out of the blue, he turns up at the library one morning. I remember when you called the station. At the time you claimed he had wandered in...but he didn't, did he?"

I walked back to the couch and sat. "If you read from those private files on Mark Ellison, you have a fair idea of what happened."

Zakary waved that away. "I would actually like to hear about it from your perspective."

"Marta Ellison was one of the darker magickal practitioners, it has been my misfortune to encounter," I said, folding my hands in my lap. "I'd had my eye on her after she and her family first moved to Ames Crossing. The village is small, and people talk."

"She wasn't a very nice woman," Zakary agreed.

I smirked at his bland description. "There's an understatement If I ever heard one. There was a nasty string of...*events*, shall we say, around Marta. From her thirty-five-year-old boss having a sudden heart attack and her taking over his job, to a house catching fire that just happened to belong to a neighbor she didn't get along with. Right down to the childcare worker who was in a serious car accident after reporting suspicious bruises on Mark at his day care."

Zakary nodded. "I knew about the report on Mark, it's what the husband used to push for sole custody. But as to the day care worker, I thought that accident was a coincidence."

I pushed my glasses back up my nose. "In my world, Zakary, there is no such thing as coincidence."

He leaned back. "So how did you find the boy?"

"Magick, especially dark magick, leaves a trace. I followed it and eventually found Marta and her son. She was hiding in a cave along the cliffs." I hesitated and chose my next words with care. "After dealing with Marta, I picked up the child and got him out, and brought him back to my home."

"Why didn't you call Sherriff Randall, or take the boy to a hospital?" His tone was curious, not angry or accusatory.

"I took him to my home because there are some injuries, that a modern medical team would be unable to treat."

"Are we talking about psychic injuries?" Zakary asked. "Similar to the type that Chauncey Marquette suffered?"

I nodded. "The child was in a trance-like state when I found him. So I did the best I could to break the thrall his mother had cast over him. It wasn't easy."

I gazed at the flames in the fireplace and recalled how Marta had chosen death over defeat. She'd spat one last curse at her husband and son before throwing herself from the mouth of the cave. I hadn't wasted time trying to save her. Breaking the curse had taken immediate action and an incredible amount of work. But it had been absolutely worth it. I smiled to myself, recalling Mark's happy face when he'd shown off his first missing tooth to me at the library earlier today.

"I remember when we arrived at the library you were white as a ghost," Zakary said. "At the time, I thought it was because you were shaken that the boy had wandered in."

"Honestly, the bigger the magick the more it costs the practitioner, physically. It can make your blood sugar crash, drain and exhaust you."

Zakary narrowed his eyes as he thought it over. "You took a few days off after the boy was found. I remember."

"My fatigue was more from battling his psychotic mother and breaking her death curse, than from doing the healing work on the child," I said bluntly.

"Death curse?" Zakary's eyebrows went way up. "Are you serious?"

I didn't blink. "Deadly serious."

"I'm sorry. Your words simply caught me off guard." He blew out a long breath. "Could you please explain what you meant when you said that you *battled* his mother?"

"It was a magickal battle," I said. "What did you think happened, Zakary? That I climbed in that cave and said, 'pretty please', and she simply handed over her son without a fight?"

"Was it like the magick I saw with Chauncey?"

"No," I sighed. "This was different, but it was still intense."

"Does the boy remember any of it?" Zakary sounded worried for the child.

"No," I reached out and laid my fingers on his arm. "He remembers nothing except waking up in the library and me holding him in my lap until the EMS and Sherriff arrived."

Zakary gently covered my hand with his. "That was incredibly kind."

"It's simply what I do," I said. "I swore an oath, to protect and to help the inhabitants of Ames Crossing. That vow comes first, before anything else."

"I understand," Zakary said. "You protect and serve, too. I'm sorry that it took me a while to come to terms with all of this." He gently rubbed the back of my hand. "I've missed you, Amanda. So much."

"I've missed you too, and I'm sorry that I was forced to keep my heritage a secret from you," I said. "I hated doing it, but there are precious few who can accept the truth about the darker things that I deal with, and I felt that maintaining—"

"Your cover?" Zakary said.

"My cover," I agreed. "That it would be the best way to keep you safe."

Zakary sat there holding my hands and studying my face intently. "Is that why you kept me at arms length? You were trying to keep *me* safe?"

"It was one of the reasons," I said. "I am truly sorry that you misinterpreted my caution for inexperience. That wasn't the way *I* wanted it to be, Zakary. However, it wouldn't have been fair to have started a physical relationship with you, when you had no idea who I truly was."

"That, and you would never have been able to hide the tattoos." He said with the smallest of smiles. "Even you couldn't have pulled that off."

I lifted my brows. "Oh ye of little faith. I'll have you know that I had about a half dozen scenarios worked out. I could have pulled it off, beautifully."

"Really?" He started to grin. "Had it all worked out, did you?"

I tried not to smile. "I did."

"So, are we talking like erotic fantasies?"

"Deputy, you have *no* idea," I said straight-faced. "Maybe I'll tell you about it some time."

"Okay," he said cheerfully, tugging me closer. "What do you say? Let's start over. Right now."

I let out a breath I hadn't been aware I'd been holding. "I'd like that."

We slowly leaned into each other and the kiss was warm and sweet. Somehow it felt like the first one we'd ever truly shared.

After a moment he pulled back. "Hi, I'm Zakary," he said holding out a hand for me to shake. "I'm a deputy with the Sherriff's department, and I coach the high school basketball team. My hobbies include hiking, camping, and fishing. I also have this thing for smart, mysterious, and spooky red-heads."

"Hello," I said, shaking his hand. "I'm Amanda, and I am the Ames Crossing head librarian and Guardian. My hobbies include, reading, cooking, battling evil and removing serious paranormal threats. *I* have a taste for the strong, kind, handsome, boy-next-door types."

Zakary grinned over my description of him. "I think if this relationship is to go any further, we should put all our cards on the table," he said.

"Full transparency." I nodded. "That is very wise."

He pulled me close. "Now, in order for there to be no more secrets between us, I think— strictly for safety reasons—that you should show me some of those scenarios, you mentioned a bit ago."

I peered over the top of my glasses. "I wouldn't want to frighten you, Deputy."

"I'm tough." He nipped my bottom lip. "I can take it."

"In that case." I kissed him quickly and stood. "Why don't you follow me upstairs? We should probably check the bedroom anyway, and make sure there is nothing dangerous lurking about."

He stood. "Roger that."

Together, with laughter, we went up the stairs hand in hand.

CHAPTER TWELVE

I woke up the next morning to a gorgeous, naked, man in my bed. Since his nose was about four inches from mine I could see him quite clearly, even without my glasses on. I studied his handsome face, thought back to our activities the night before, and smiled.

His eyes popped open. "Morning," he said softly.

"Good morning."

"Come over here," he said, pulling me close so my head was on his shoulder.

"How are you feeling?" I asked him.

"Relaxed." he sighed deeply.

I slid my hand down and was delighted to discover that the term 'relaxed' was highly inaccurate. "This doesn't feel *relaxed* to me," I said giving him a gentle squeeze.

He rolled me under him and settled between my legs. "How does *this* feel?" he asked, pressing forward.

"Like I have your full attention." I said, wrapping myself around him.

Later that morning, I waved goodbye to him from the back deck as he left for work. We had turned a corner in our relationship, and I wasn't sure who was more surprised by that, him or me.

After a final wave, I ducked back inside to the warmth of the house. I had work to do. Luckily I had the day off, because there was the insurance company to call, and a repairman to hire so the doors on the house would close properly.

I stopped and filled up the kettle for tea, put it on the stove, and hurried into the living room for my list. I came up short when I saw the three Phalaenopsis orchids Drusilla had tended to. The plants had shot out new growth over night and were on the verge of blooming again.

"That's some impressive earth magick," I said. Drusilla had left the plants lined up on the dining room table, and I bent over the plants to take a closer look. I gasped when one of the buds trembled, and slowly, right before my eyes began to bloom.

***

After breakfast, I got the process started with the insurance company, but before I could put in a call to a handyman, Jeremiah Ames knocked on my kitchen door.

"Heard you needed some help," he said stepping over the threshold, and his wife Jenna was right behind him and carrying a covered dish.

"Hi sweetie!" Jenna said. "Don't you worry, my Jeremiah can fix anything."

"Well, thank you," I managed.

"Of course. What are friends for?" she said as she slipped a casserole into my refrigerator.

I'd worked with her for three years, we had a casual sort of work friendship, but having her show up ready to work, and bringing food, made me realize what a treasure she truly was. The woman stood there in a loud holiday sweater, her silver hair pulled back in a neat ponytail and jingle bell earrings chimed at her ears. "Now," she said rubbing her hands together. "How can I help?"

Thanks to the Ames', by late that afternoon both of the doors had been repaired and new deadbolts were installed—I figured they might as well, I wasn't sure if the wards would ever go back to their original operating strength. Jenna had made a run to the store with my list and came back with the dry goods and personal products that had been destroyed.

She even surprised me by hitting up a home décor store in Alton and snagging ornaments for my tree, and some new holiday décor, greenery, and lights for the mantle.

"It was all on clearance!" she announced. "I saw you used blues, so I found these midnight blue and silver ornaments."

"Well, thank you," I said, touched by the thoughtfulness of the gesture.

"Not a lot of lights left, but I did find these tiny blue ones...thought they might look good in the pine garland on the mantle."

I'd never used blue lights, but her enthusiasm

was contagious. "Wonderful," I said.

"And I bought this mercury glass looking reindeer..."

"Good god, woman!" Jeremiah called from the kitchen. "Any excuse to decorate."

"Oh hush, you!" she called back.

"This is fabulous. Thank you, Jenna." I smiled over the reindeer. "I *will* put this on my mantle."

When all was said and done, I wasn't sure who had more fun re-decorating the living room for the holidays, her or me. Besides, she was right. The decorations she'd bought worked out better than the original ones had. Once we had the new garland in place and lit, I gave her a one-armed hug and told her I was going to let her choose all of my holiday décor from now on.

Zakary arrived with a bottle of wine and a pizza, right in time to see the Ames' leaving for the day.

"I'll call you when that seeded glass comes in," Jeremiah said.

"Thank you," I said, as Zakary greeted the couple.

"I bet my old contractor friend can get that glass pretty quickly for you," Jeremiah said, holding the new door for his wife. "Then we'll get it installed in the cabinets."

"I appreciate it. How much do I owe you for everything?"

"You just cover the cost of the supplies, the new doors and such," he said. "I'm not charging you for labor."

"Mr. Ames," I began.

"If you want to pay me, you can invite us to dinner when this is all done. Grill me a big steak or something and we'll call it even."

"Deal," I said and held out my hand.

"See you at work." Jenna gave me a hug after I'd shaken her husband's hand, and they left, arm in arm.

I smiled over the older couple as they left.

Zakary set the food down, walked directly to me, and pulled me in close for a kiss. "I'd ask how today went, but I can see that for myself."

"The house is starting to feel like it used to," I said, and on cue the kitchen lights became brighter, there was a burst of cinnamon fragrance on the air, and the atmosphere became cozier.

Zakary stopped and looked up at the lights. "Umm...is it my imagination or did the house actually respond to what you said?"

I smiled. "Why don't we open that bottle of wine you brought, go sit by the fireplace, and I'll tell you all about it."

We spent a cozy night by the fire, eating pizza and drinking wine, while I explained to Zakary about the wards that had been originally placed on the house.

"*That's* what you meant when you said the house had an advanced security system," he sipped his wine and thought it over.

"There's more," I said, wanting everything to be out in the open at last.

Nyx's climbed on his lap and he gave her a scratch under the chin. "Go ahead, Amanda. I'm listening."

I explained about the magick that had been a part of the house itself. I briefly described to him some of the work that had been done to turn it to positive—as opposed to negative. I also spoke about the workroom in the cellar *and* what it currently held. He remained silent, waiting until I had finished.

"Wow," he blew out a long breath. "Those old stories they tell kids about the bad witch in the village *are* actually true."

"Louisa Midnight Beaumont, was the impetus—the reason behind my family becoming Guardians."

"She was that bad?"

"She was. I told Estella once to think of Louisa's magick like a toxin that had affected the environment, slowly poisoning everything around it."

"So if I understand you correctly, then Marta Ellison was attracted here, to Ames Crossing, because of the evil energy that still hangs around?"

"Exactly." I nodded. "My job will never be truly finished, Zakary. It's important that you understand that."

"And because of the damage Louisa inflicted, her son and his descendants took on the task of cleaning up her mess," Zakary said.

"Or maintaining it as best they could. But that darkness will always attract evil, and there will continue to be situations that require—"

"Your expertise?" he said.

"Precisely."

"Can you give me some examples?"

"Well, there was an entity causing problems at the antique store last month."

"Hey, I took that call." He frowned. "So it wasn't malicious mischief?"

"No," I said, taking his hand. "It was something else."

Zakary shook his head. "Maybe I'm better off *not* knowing everything."

"Could you simply agree not to know?" I asked.

"I think that may be the only fair way for you and I to go forward. After all, I can't discuss the details of my cases with civilians either." He gave my hand a gentle squeeze. "Can I ask one you final thing?"

"Yes?"

"Are you sure the spirit of Pierre-Michel Marquette didn't cause the damage to your house?"

"I'm sure. He's contained."

"You know, I wondered what had happened to that portrait..." Zakary said. "Sherriff Randall said it had been *secured*, but I didn't know exactly what that meant."

"To be clear, you are the only other person who knows where the portrait is. Not even Leroy knows. I did that for—"

"Security reasons." Zakary finished. "And I agree with you. How long *are* you going to keep his portrait down there?"

"Philippe asked for time," I explained. "Time to decide what to do about the painting. It's fairly valuable and an important part of his family's history."

Zakary tossed back the last of his wine. "Maybe he should burn the sucker."

"I suggested that," I said. "Fire would be one sure way of destroying the portal and banishing the spirit once and for all."

Zakary shrugged. "You're the expert."

I smiled. "I do my best."

***

The holidays passed, and I divided my time between Zakary and the Midnight family. Leroy returned home from his trip and teased me unmercifully about the new dynamic of my relationship with the deputy. I'd have worried if he hadn't. Leroy told me he thinks that 'the boy' has potential. As for Zakary, he's slowly warming up to Leroy.

Camilla Midnight-Ames dropped by the library one January afternoon with the photocopied pages from Victoria Midnight's journal put together in a three-ring binder.

"Every page is there," she said showing me the binder, "and I put notes at the bottom of the page for you."

"You color coded them." I nodded. "Thank you. That will certainly save me time."

"At last!" Camilla laughed. "Someone who appreciates my organizational skills." Camilla checked her watch. "My lunch break is over. I need to head back to the shop so Estella can go to lunch."

I closed the binder and set it on my desk. "Thank you for this, Camilla, it's wonderful."

She gave my hand a squeeze. "You're welcome, cousin. See you later."

I walked her out, and was caught by a few patrons. By the time I returned to my office I opened the door and discovered that the notebook was lying open on my desk. I knew that no one had gone into my office. I'd been standing in full sight of the one and only door the entire time. Yet there the binder lay, open on the table.

The sacred runes and sigils tattooed on my back prickled in a warning. I took a deep breath, and shut the door. Squaring my shoulders, I walked over to my desk and sat. Nothing else had been disturbed on the surface of the desk. My cell phone still rested beside it, and I got the oddest feeling of déjà vu.

Carefully I tugged the binder closer and read the entry.

Stolen away to be claimed by those who had none,
The most precious of gifts, shining bright like the sun.
I watch from afar, helpless, as the lie flourishes and grows,
While they live content in a house made of darkness and shadows.
This heritage of secrets will be passed down through the years,

Generations of evil that no one should have to bear.
When the Spring equinox moon turns to ash, all wrongs will be made right,
Revealed by a shining star, and a wise, brave daughter of midnight.

The entry was marked as 'random poetry', but I also saw that Estella had scribbled a note at the bottom of the photocopied page. The note read: *This one gives me the creeps. Is she mentioning me again?*

My cell phone chimed, and I glanced at it and saw I had an update from the DNA kit that I'd sent in with Estella. I picked up the phone, tapped the screen and read the notice that my sample was being processed. I could expect results in about two weeks.

Deliberately, I closed the binder, put it away in a drawer and locked it. I'd take the pages home tonight and study the writings in private. Now, I had the children's reading hour to oversee.

As January rolled on toward February, Zakary and I spent more and more time together. My life was settling into a new sort of routine, and it made me happy to be with someone who could not only accept my heritage and the obligations it entailed, but who shared my sense of duty to the community.

Zakary invited me to attend one of his team's home basketball games, and while I could admit that basketball had never really been my thing, I did enjoy the action, and of course it was sort of sentimental seeing the students cheer at my alma mater. The high school band still played the same fight song, and the cheers hadn't changed that much.

I enjoyed watching Zakary coach the boys much more than the game itself, truth be told. I studied him as he paced up and down the side of the court. There he was, my boy-next-door, handsome, blue-eyed man. He was kind, caring, had a good sense of humor, and he was delightfully imaginative in the bedroom.

I sighed. Zakary Parker just ticked all the boxes for me. I was a lucky woman to have him back in my life. I was falling in love, and I hoped that he would soon return my affections.

I simply needed to be patient, I reminded myself. *I had to be. I'd come too close to losing him to rush things now.*

I was jolted out of my musings by a familiar voice. "Scoot over, *chica.*"

"Estella," I laughed. "What are you doing here?"

"Tracking you down," she said, squeezing herself onto the bleacher beside me.

"Why? Is something wrong?"

She shook her head. "You gotta learn to check your damn phone more often."

"What?" I said over the crowd.

"Your phone," she said again. "The DNA tests results are in."

"Oh, okay," I said, and pulled up the app on my phone.

"See? There's your ethnicity estimate." She pointed out the data.

I read the numbers. "Forty-one percent Germanic Europe and Midwestern United States. Thirty percent England, Wales and Northwestern Europe. Eleven percent Ireland and Scotland." I laughed. "Ha! Scotland, who knew?"

"Aye, lassie," Estella said in a passible brogue.

"Oh and I'm eighteen percent French." I laughed at the surprise. "*French*? Where did the French come from?"

She grinned. "It's a mystery."

"Let me see your numbers," I said. We spent the break between periods looking at each other's numbers. Estella had an amazing mixture of Europe, Midwestern United States, England, and Wales, from the Midnight family. From her mother there was Mexico, and a dash of Native American.

"See?" She held up her phone. "If you look in the section where it says 'Matches', you and I are listed as fourth cousins."

"That's great!" I smiled. "I'll look at it more when I get home later."

"I can't wait to show the family," she said.

The basketball game resumed, so we put our phones away and I switched my focus to watching Zakary coach the game.

And then I completely forgot all about those DNA results.

***

March had arrived, but you'd never know it by looking out the windows. There was yet another snowstorm predicted and the temperatures hovered in the low 20's. Despite the weather forecast, I'd been invited to a party, and I had every intention of going. Danielle Marquette was about to celebrate her first birthday, and I wouldn't miss it for the world. Over the past few months I'd become friendly with all of the daughters of Midnight.

"Are you sure it's safe to go up to the mansion tonight?" Zakary sat on the edge of the bed, watching me get dressed.

"Why?" I asked. I stood in my bra and tugged my long blue wool skirt in place. "Worried about the possibility of more ghouls and ghosts?"

"Well..." he drug the word out. "There is a full moon out tonight."

"I'll protect you," I pulled my black sweater over my head and smoothed it down.

"Speaking of protection," he said. "Are you wearing your blade tonight?"

I pulled my boots out of the closet and went over to sit beside him on the bed. "What do you think?" I said, hiking up my skirt and flashing the holster that was strapped to my upper thigh.

"God damn," he breathed. "That is so *hot*."

I unzipped my boots and began to slip them on. "There was a time you didn't consider it to be so."

He reached over and grabbed a handful of my hair. Playfully, he pulled me back by it. "How am I supposed to focus on a kid's birthday party when I know you have that on underneath that skirt?" His voice was almost a growl.

"Be brave, Deputy. Think of your duty."

His started to grin. "Smart ass."

"Why yes I am." I stood up. "You'd be amazed at the things you can learn by reading. There was an excellent book that arrived at the library today..."

He stood with a groan of frustration. "Unless you are going to tell me the book was the *Kama Sutra* I don't want to talk about books right now."

I slid my glasses down and considered him from over the rims. "It might interest you to know that I have read that particular tome."

"Sweet Jesus!"

"It would be safe to say that he has nothing to do with it." When he stared, I smiled. "I promise to show you later."

"This is going to be a long night," Zakary groused as we prepared to leave.

An hour later, and I stood in the big open space that comprised the kitchen, dining room and family room in the family wing of the mansion. There were fourteen adults and four children present. Danielle sat in her high chair stripped down to a diaper and undershirt, frowning at the miniature cake her mother had made for her.

She tentatively stuck a finger in the icing and looked up in confusion at her parents.

"Dive in, baby girl," Gabriella urged her.

Her great-grandfather, Henri Marquette, sat in a chair off to her side. He murmured something to the baby in French, and she began to grin. A second later she slapped her hands on the cake and icing went everywhere.

"For gods sake!" Gabriella rolled her eyes. "I think the baby actually understood him."

Philippe began to laugh. "She's bilingual."

Gabriella served slices from a separate cake to the rest of the guests. Estella was scooping ice cream, and Brooke was passing the slices around.

I sat at the dining room table with Estella and her grandmother. My friend was currently trying to talk Priscilla into doing a DNA test, too. "It would be a more modern way to track the family tree you're so obsessed with," Estella argued.

A moment later Henri Marquette joined us, and pulled a chair up next to me. He smoothly introduced himself and listened as Estella kept up her argument with her grandmother.

"I have done that DNA kit to track the Marquette family line," he said. "I have the app on my phone as well."

"Ah-ha!" Estella pounced on that. "See? Technology is awesome. You might learn something surprising about your own family." Estella was thrilled to discover that Henri had done the same kit she had.

I watched as Zakary stood and talked to Max Dubois, Jacob and Jaime Ames. He listened to whatever the child was saying and seemed to be enjoying himself.

He'll make a wonderful father someday, I thought. I caught myself and reined those thoughts in. Then I heard Estella...

"Yeah, it was a big surprise, Amanda discovered she had Scotland and France in her ethnicity estimate and she never even knew."

"France?" Henri smiled at me.

"Show him, Amanda," Estella urged.

I pulled my phone from my purse. "Yes, it certainly was news to me. I suppose I should look into it more. But I hadn't bothered with it. I don't have very many close relatives."

"But you do have us," Gabriella said from across the kitchen.

"Fourth cousins not withstanding," I agreed.

Estella grabbed my phone. "You never even checked your matches, did you?"

"I filled in my family tree while I waited for the results." I said. "All the way back to Louisa Midnight and Eugene Beaumont. It wasn't hard." I shrugged. "Lots of only children—all boys—and they were all named Victor. My father is Victor Beaumont the fourth."

With a few touches Estella had the screen to

the 'matches' section. "See, here I am, it says fourth cousin." She grinned and held the phone up for the room to see. "Girl, you got a bunch of matches! So much for the theory that you don't have very many relatives..." she frowned and pulled the screen even closer to her face.

"Do you need glasses?" I teased her.

"Um, no. But I think you *really* need to take a look at your matches."

"Why?" For a split second I thought she was going to tell me I was related to Zakary.

"Mr. Marquette?" Estella said. "Would you pull up the matches on your cell phone?"

He didn't argue, and Estella's tone of voice had everyone falling silent. Estella handed me my phone and pointed to the screen. "Look what that says. Right there at the top."

"Henri Marquette, distant cousin," I read.

He held up his phone and showed me his matches. I checked the app on my phone again. Henri Marquette was listed as: distant cousin. Confidence: Good. Possible range 5th to 8th cousin.

"How can we possibly be related?" I wondered out loud.

CHAPTER THIRTEEN

Before anything else could be said, the lights began to flicker. I felt the drop in the barometric pressure. It hit me square in the center of my chest. Beside me Estella stood up and reached for Chauncey. He grabbed her arm and they stood together.

"Aw, come on!" Gabriella said. "I suppose it's too much to ask that my daughter's birthday be ghost free?"

The lights in the kitchen went out, and all the sacred symbols on my skin flared to life. I rose to my feet, and Zakary came immediately to my side.

"Everyone stay calm," I said.

The temperature dropped dramatically and, sensing the direction of the manifestation, I shifted my attention. Just in time to see that a figure had begun to coalesce in the hallway.

"Here it comes." Camilla's voice was excited, but not frightened.

A light was moving down the hall and closer towards the room where the family had gathered. From my vantage point I could clearly see the spirit. Her hair was dark red, and she wore that same yellow dress I'd seen her in before.

"My god," Zakary's voice was ragged as the apparition floated in the doorway.

"Hello, Victoria." I said, calmly, over the gasps of the people behind me.

"Now you know the truth." Her voice whispered through the room and the scent of lilacs wafted after it. "I am yours, and you are *his*." She reached out a hand. "Stolen away to be claimed by those who had none. I watched from afar, helpless, as the lie flourished and grew... Then they sent me away."

The hair rose on the back of my neck. *I knew those words.* She was quoting from her own prophecy. "What was stolen, Victoria?" I asked, even though I had an awful feeling that I already knew.

"The babe," she said.

"Victor," I said as the pieces all fell into place. "Victor Eugene Beaumont was not Louisa's child. He was *your* child."

"Never hers," she said. "You belong to Pierre-Michel, and to me." With a sad smile, she faded away.

The lights bounced back on. The babies began to babble and coo like nothing had happened, and the rest of us stood there, staring at each other. Then everyone began to speak at once.

***

The party, not surprisingly, had ended shortly after the ghostly visit.

Now, it was past midnight. I was back in my own home and was sitting elbow-to-elbow at my dining room table with Zakary. At the moment all my research into the Beaumont family tree was spread across the table. Zakary was leafing through the three-ring binder Camilla had given me, and I had even pulled a journal of Louisa's from the period of time when her son had been born...

If he'd even actually been *her* son at all. I took notes on a yellow legal pad, and the more I dug into this mystery the deeper my heart sank. After a couple hours of research I had my answer, and it broke my heart.

I had been completely blinded by what I *thought* I knew about my own personal history. Pierre-Michel had shouted at me that night at the mansion. He'd said: '*It's a lie! You are mine, not hers*!' And at the time my focus had been on rescuing Chauncey from the possession...so I hadn't paid much attention to what the spirit had said.

Well, I thought, *I was certainly paying attention now.*

"Zakary," I asked. "Would you read that prophecy about the Spring Moon, out loud to me, again?"

He flipped right to the page. "Stolen away to be claimed by those who had none," he began, "the most precious of gifts, shining bright like the sun. I watch from afar, helpless, as the lie flourishes and grows, while they live content in a house made of darkness and shadows. This heritage of secrets will be passed down through the years, generations of evil that no one should have to bear. When the Spring equinox moon turns to ash, all wrongs will be made right. Revealed by a shining star, and a wise, brave daughter of midnight."

"That prophecy is eerily accurate," I admitted.

"Tonight is the full moon and I guess you could call it the spring moon, since the equinox is in a week." He frowned. "I don't get the 'turns to ash' part though."

"The Celtic lunar calendar assigns a tree to each full moon of the year. The 'Ash Moon' is assigned to a full moon that falls between February 18 and March 17."

"And you just knew that?"

I looked up from my notes. "It's fairly common knowledge in occult circles."

"Ever since we got home you've been hitting these old books and taking notes like crazy. What have you discovered?"

"I have confirmed the dates on Victor the first's birth, which was April 10, 1848 and

Pierre-Michel's death, on October 31, 1847."

Zakary counted on his fingers. "Meaning Pierre-Michel *could* have been the father of Victoria's baby."

"Correct. I also found the mentions of the birth of the child, the death of Louisa's husband, plus when she'd had Victoria committed."

"Super librarian to the rescue!" Zakary leaned over and kissed my cheek. "So what's your theory?"

I pulled my glasses off and rubbed my eyes. "I'm afraid it is not a very pleasant one."

Zakary rubbed a hand across my shoulder. "Well I sort of figured that when Victoria said they had stolen the baby away."

I slipped my glasses back on. "Louisa mentions in her journals that she did everything including spells to try and conceive, but that after five years together she and Eugene remained childless." I pushed the journal closer to Zakary. "Look, she even wrote about how she and her husband offered to buy a baby from a local woman who already had six. Louisa wasn't happy when the woman turned them down."

Zakary whistled. "Holy crap."

"She also had several pages devoted to the curse she unleashed on Pierre-Michel for not only dallying with her sister, Victoria, but also for being suspected in the death of his wife, Bridgette." When he leaned forward as if to look for those notes, I shut the journal. "Trust me, you don't want to see those."

"You said it was Mary Ames, Bridgette's sister, that had paid for the curse, right?"

"Yes." I nodded. "So let's imagine that Victoria is distraught and mourning over the death of her lover for a few months. If we do the math, by then she'd have been about five months along and unable to hide her pregnancy. Which would have been a huge scandal back in the day. Not only Victoria's reputation, but that of her entire family would have been ruined. And if you stop and consider that the father of her child was a married man, and a suspected murderer, it would have horrified the entire Midnight family."

"Meaning they *had* to keep it a secret." Zakary rubbed a hand over his chin. "I'm betting Louisa saw an opportunity to keep the family's good name, and to finally get her hands on a baby...so she took advantage of it."

I tapped a pen against my notebook while I thought it over. "That makes sense. She took Victoria into her home—telling the family it was to help with her melancholia—but it was actually to hide her sister's pregnancy from the public. Meaning Louisa would have had to have faked a pregnancy for herself."

"Like a pillow baby-bump thing," Zakary guessed.

"Probably," I agreed. "That way when the baby was born, she could claim it was hers."

"Who would have delivered the baby?" Zakary asked.

"It's a safe bet that Louisa delivered him. Because Victor the first, was born in this house, in April of 1848. And since Victoria was living with them, she would have been there to have privately nursed the baby for his first year."

"That's horrible!" Zakary said. "They used her like a brood mare."

"According to the timeline, Eugene died when Victor was a little over a year old. A few months after that, Louisa had Victoria committed to an asylum."

"That way *no one* would ever know the truth about the child." Zakary sadly shook his head.

I nodded in agreement. "And after everything she'd endured, Victoria completely lost her grip on reality."

"I bet Louisa played that up," Zakary grumbled.

"She did. It's in her journals, I suppose she was trying to convince herself of how noble she was." I sighed. "But with Victoria out of the way, the truth about Victor's parentage was kept a secret for over one hundred and seventy years."

"Until you did that DNA test."

"That was Estella's idea, and I think she was trying to push me into revealing my links to the Midnight family—"

"Amanda," Zakary interrupted. "When exactly did you mail out the DNA test?

"Back in December..." I trailed off as it hit me. "The night before the house was vandalized."

"Clearly someone or something wasn't

happy about you sending off that test."

"Because it would reveal the truth about my ancestry. That I'm a Marquette, not a Beaumont."

"Is it possible that Pierre-Michel somehow escaped the confinement and did all that to get your attention?"

"No," I said. "My containment is still holding. I checked again tonight when I went down to the cellar to retrieve Louisa's journal from the safe. Believe me, I'd know if his spirit had escaped."

"If it wasn't Pierre-Michel who did all the damage at your house, then who was it?" Zakary asked.

"My money is on Louisa," I said. "This house was her original power base. It was foolish of me not to expect that some of her presence might have remained." I rubbed my forehead as I thought it over. "She had a reputation for being vindictive, and it would also explain why the house is slow to come back to its full strength."

"Maybe her ghost didn't go in the cellar because of its close proximity to Pierre-

Michel," Zakary said.

"That's possible."

"It would make sense," Zakary agreed. "You mailed off the kits, and Louisa's spirit loses it and her anger tears up the place. But she can't or won't go in the cellar because that's where *he* is contained and you've got all that spook-fighting equipment down there."

"I do believe you are correct, sir." I winked at him and began tidying up the papers and books.

Zakary yawned. "Let's go to bed."

"As soon as I secure Louisa's papers," I said. "I can't have my evil ancestor's..."

Zakary ran his hand down my hair. "But she's *not* yours. Victoria was your however-many-greats grandmother. You aren't descended from evil, old Louisa. You and your dad came from Pierre-Michel and Victoria. A couple that loved each other so much that even death hasn't stopped them from helping their current descendants."

I stopped what I was doing to study him. "You are a good man, Zakary. That was a lovely thing to say, and what I most needed to hear."

He smiled and pulled me close.

I snuggled my head on his chest, and then I took a chance. "I love you," I whispered.

"I love you too." Zakary's arms tightened around me. "I think we make a pretty good team."

I lifted my face to his. "We do."

He dropped a quick kiss on my mouth. "Maybe we could work together on cases, from time to time."

"I suppose we could," I agreed. "We should probably lay out some sort of guidelines, and rules for any future paranormal cases that we decide to work on together—"

My words were cut off when he pressed his lips to mine. After a moment I forgot what I'd even been saying.

"Amanda?" His voice was low. "How long will it take you to secure those journals?"

I smiled. "Only a few minutes."

"I'm not waiting that long to have you," he said and nudged me to lie back on the dining room table.

"We can't!" I laughed up at him. "Not on top of the books!"

"Wanna bet?" he said, shoving the books out of the way.

***

The next afternoon I sat at the table in the conference room at the Marquette mansion. I had called a meeting with the Marquette family, and I'd also asked Estella to join us. I sat on one side of the table with Estella and Gabriella flanking me, and across from us sat Henri, Philippe and Chauncey Marquette.

I had the papers and copies of my research to show them all, and I shared with them my theory of how Louisa had managed to pass off Victoria's child as her own, thus keeping the secret hidden for several generations.

Gabriella held Danielle on her lap and lifted tear-filled eyes to me. "This is all so sad, I can't imagine one sister doing that to another."

"I didn't show you this to upset you, Gabriella," I said briskly. "I am sharing this information with all of you because according to the DNA tests and the paperwork I've found, I am in fact related to the Marquettes—as well as the Midnights."

Danielle squealed happily.

I smiled and touched my fingertip to Danielle's button nose. "You said it, cousin."

Estella drummed her fingers on the table. "No wonder the ghosts have been working so hard to get our attention."

"What will you do with the portrait of Pierre-Michel?" Philippe asked. "Is it safe to return it to the mansion?"

"No, I don't believe that it is," I said. "The spirit was too violent the last time we encountered it."

"Being accused of murder and having your child stolen away, might make the guy a bit pissed off," Gabriella said dryly.

"Yeah, well, you're not Pierre-Michel's chosen target, are you?" Estella argued.

"Hold it," I said as everyone began to argue. "For everyone's safety the painting should remained contained."

Chauncey's shoulders dropped in relief. "I agree," he said.

Philippe held up a hand for peace. "I too, agree with Amanda. The portrait will remain where it is. That way it can cause no further harm."

"Hey, I don't want it back in my house," Gabriella said shifting the baby. "I was only saying, now we know why the ghost is lashing out."

"Well, if that is all?" I stood and pushed the paperwork into a neat stack. "These copies are for you, Mr. Marquette, for your own genealogy research." I handed the stack over to the older gentleman. "My father's contact information is in there as well. I spoke to him this morning, and brought him up to speed. He's looking forward to meeting all of you."

"*Merci beaucoup.*" Henri accepted the papers with a smile. "I look forward to speaking to him."

I managed to make my way around the table but found my way blocked by all three Marquette men.

Henri held out his arms silently. "Allow me to formally welcome you to the Marquette family, *cousine.*"

"Oh." I hadn't expected that. I accepted the warm hug and gave him one in return. "Thank you, Mr. Marquette."

"Henri," he corrected. "You may call me Henri." He looked to his grandsons. "Go on, say hello to your *cousine*."

Philippe grinned. "Welcome to the family." He gave me a formal kiss on the cheek.

I laughed and accepted a friendly hug from Chauncey next. "Nice to know we have a paranormal expert in the family," he said.

"I hope you won't ever need my services ever again," I said, sincerely.

"Me too." Chauncey winked.

After a few moments I said my goodbyes, and the Marquettes all went back to their day.

Estella walked me out to my car. It was breezy but the sun was shining warmly. "So much for your theory that you don't have very many relatives," she said dryly.

I tossed my hair out of my face. "My father was beyond excited when I told him about everything this morning. He and Mom are coming up in a few weeks to visit, and he can't wait to meet everyone."

"Vic is coming up from Florida?" Estella grinned. "I can't wait to meet him, either!"

"Estella?" I stopped and reached back for her hand. "I wanted to say thank you. For everything. Thanks for being my friend."

"Back at ya." She gave my fingers a light squeeze.

"I don't know what I would have done without you these past few months."

"Hey, somebody had to kick you up to the line."

I laughed. "I suppose that's true."

I took a moment and studied the three-story gothic stone mansion. After two hundred years it still stood. It had seen war, tragedy, and then a revival, happiness and love. My ancestors had lived and died there. Three of my cousins had married there, and now Philippe and Gabriella were raising their family within its walls. It was humbling to realize that I was playing a part in its continuing story as well.

The old stone house had, in its own way, transformed my life. I'd met Estella there and gained a true friend. Because of her, my heritage as a daughter of Midnight was no longer hidden. Zakary had finally discovered the truth about my role as a Guardian within those walls, and recently a secret about my *own* ancestry had been brought out in the light of day.

I was both a Marquette and a daughter of Midnight. The mansion had, in one way or another, simply changed everything.

"What are you thinking?" Estella asked me as I stood there lost in my own thoughts.

"I'm thinking that this old house still holds many secrets. I wonder if we'll ever know them all?"

Estella frowned. "And I'm supposed to find that comforting?"

I grinned. "Don't worry, cousin, I've got your back."

She rolled her eyes. "Get out of here. Go home, find that hot deputy, and wear him out or something."

"What an excellent idea." I smiled. "I believe I'll go do that."

The End

Turn the page for a sneak peek of the final book in the *Daughters of Midnight* series.
Book 6, *Midnight Destiny*

Midnight Destiny

Book 6 in the *Daughters Of Midnight* series

The kicky breeze that whipped through the cottage gardens of the Marquette mansion was a sure sign of change. There was the slightest chill in the September air, and it was a welcome signal that the summer had at last caved in to fall. I lifted my face to the fresh air and breathed it in.

I walked along with my eighteen-month-old niece, Danielle, and considered all of the changes in my life. It had been a year since I had tossed my belongings in a duffle bag, hopped on a plane, and flown clear across the country to meet the family I'd never known I had. The culture shock in coming from California and moving to a historic—and haunted—small town had been huge.

Twelve months later and I felt right at home. More than I ever had bopping around the world as an Air Force brat. Who would've ever thought that I, Estella Flores Midnight, would end up in Illinois, living in a spooky little village.

However, I wasn't alone. It still surprised me to wake up and realize I had a grandmother, three sisters, three brother-in-laws, a nephew and nieces. Oh, and a cousin. The wish I'd made on my birthday the year before had come true. I had a family, a big one, and I wasn't alone. Not anymore.

While the baby toddled, I followed her around making sure she didn't get into too much trouble. The kid was a pistol. She darted here and there, exclaiming over every flower and every leaf she saw. I didn't dare take my eyes off her, because the kid was strong-willed and she'd already thrown a fit when I'd stopped her from finding out what the gravel on the path tasted like.

"Lala *look!*" Danielle held up a fallen oak leaf like a prize.

Lala was Danielle's version of saying Estella. I thought it was hilarious. "That's pretty," I said as she toddled over to me. I knew the drill by now. Crouching down to her level, I looked over the treasure with all the respect an eighteen-month-old would expect.

"Dat's pe-tty," Danielle agreed.

I took a moment and straightened up her tiny dark brown pigtails. Danielle allowed it, but I knew better than to fuss over her hair too long.

"Floweys!" she exclaimed, taking off to go pat the chrysanthemums blooming at the edge of the path.

"Yup," I agreed. "There are lots of flowers." I tried not to wince when she grabbed handfuls of blooms and yanked them free. There was a wedding scheduled to be held in the gardens this weekend and I'd promised Gabriella I'd keep her daughter out of the perennial beds.

While Danielle bust a gut laughing over her floweys, I sat on the edge of the grass. Worst case scenario, I decided, I'd pop over to Max's nursery and buy a few more mum plants to replace the ones Danielle was scalping. She was having way too much fun grabbing flower heads and bringing them over to me. In a few minutes I had quite the collection decorating the legs of my jeans.

Honestly, I doubted Gabriella would even

notice. Currently, my sister had a lot more on her mind than worrying over a few scalped chrysanthemums. I heard footsteps on the gravel path and turned my head. When I saw who it was, my heart gave one hard thud in reaction.

Danielle had spotted her uncle at the same time. "Cee-cee!" was toddler-speak for *Chauncey,* and Danielle promptly abandoned me to race toward him.

Chauncey stood waiting on the path and as soon as she reached him, he grabbed her and tossed her high in the air. Danielle's delighted screams filled the garden, and as I watched them both grin at each other, I was hit all over again with how damn hot he was.

He was tall with a lean build, and a head full of dark tousled hair. Between his sexy man-scruff and the light of humor in his dark eyes...it was a hell of a package.

I ought to be used to it by now. But the truth was, for the past ten months I'd been fighting my attraction to him. *We weren't well suited for each other,* I reminded myself for the thousandth time. We had nothing in common...not our backgrounds or our lifestyles. Yet I still wanted him.

To make matters worse, he'd clearly put me in the buddy category. Which made my secret physical reaction to him extremely embarrassing. The man didn't have a clue as to how I felt...and I intended to keep it that way.

I was determined to get over my desire for him. Somehow. I dug down deep and went for a casual tone of voice. "Hey," I said, while he walked over carrying Danielle.

"Hi, Aunt Lala." He glanced down at the flowers. "Weren't you supposed to keep Danielle out of the flowers while you babysat?"

"We were just pruning," I said, nonchalantly. "Tidying up the place."

Chauncey grinned at the lie. "I can always run up to the garden center and buy a couple new plants before the wedding ceremony."

I nodded. "That's exactly what I was thinking."

Danielle squirmed to be put down and Chauncey set her on her feet. The toddler immediately went right back to picking more flowers and bringing them to me.

"Have you heard anything yet?" Chauncey asked.

"Nope." I slid my phone from my pocket. "They've only been gone a couple of hours. The doctor's appointment was at two o'clock."

Chauncey sat beside me on the grass, and Danielle started bringing him flowers as well. "I guess we'll find out soon enough."

"I bet Gabriella's pregnant," I said. "She was totally green around the gills when they left for their appointment."

Chauncey grinned. "I think so too. Philippe told me Gabriella was really sick for the first few months she carried that little monster over there."

"Who's a monster, *mija*?" I asked with a playful growl in my voice.

"Lala!" Danielle whipped her head around and ran straight at me, with a growl of her own.

I absorbed the toddler tackle and let her think she'd knocked me over. "Oh no!" my voice was breathy and high as I rolled over with her on the grass. "Somebody save me from the monster!"

"I'll save you!" Chauncey's voice had me jolting and Danielle laughing.

Now, I not only had an armful of toddler, but Chauncey Marquette had grabbed me off the ground and picked us both up. Danielle thought it was great, and her laughter rolled out across the gardens. As for me, finding myself suddenly in his arms had the laughter dying in my throat.

The last thing I'd ever expected was for Chauncey to join in on the play. Now I was held close to his chest, like some heroine from a sappy romance novel. When he grinned down at me, my heart almost stopped altogether.

He wiggled his eyebrows. "You're supposed to say: 'My hero'."

It took me a moment, but I managed to roll my eyes at him. "I don't think Danielle knows those words, yet."

"My Cee-Cee!" Danielle shouted.

"That's close enough," he decided and put us both down.

I let Danielle slide out of my arms, and my eyes were helplessly locked on his. Fortunately for me, as soon as her feet hit the ground she was off and racing across the grass.

"I...I guess..." I winced over hearing myself stammer. *Get ahold of yourself!* I thought. "I'd better go and make sure she doesn't get into any trouble." I took a step back.

Chauncey stood absolutely still. "You probably should."

Something had changed. The vibes in the garden had shifted from playful to something else. Whatever it was had heat rising to my face, and my heart slamming against my ribs. My mouth went bone dry and, nervously, I licked my lips.

His eyes narrowed at the movement, and there was a look on his face...One I'd not seen before.

"I should go," I said again, inwardly cursing over sounding like a moron. "I'll, uh...see you around, Chauncey."

"See you," he said.

My face flushed, I took off after Danielle who'd shot across the lawn in search of new adventures. I absolutely refused to look over my shoulder to see if he was watching me. I had more pride than that.

I caught up to the toddler who was now pointing at a bird on a tree branch, and pride be damned, I glanced back anyway. The man was strolling down the garden path, his hands tucked in the pockets of his slacks, seemingly without a care in the world...while I stood there with my palms sweating and my heart racing.

"Damn it," I muttered. "I can put a man twice my size in a controlled hold. I can handle mean drunks in a bar, but every time Chauncey Marquette gets too close, I make a fool out of myself."

I'd known him for a year, my sister was married to his half-brother. I'd laughed with him, and helped take care of him when he'd been hurt. We'd attended weddings and family functions together, I even danced with him. Twice.

We'd kissed once, too. *But did that even count?* I wondered. Probably not. Since we'd both been possessed at the time...Now we were, friends, I supposed, and godparents to the little monster currently trying to climb up my leg.

I swung the baby up into my arms and dropped a kiss on her cheek. "What is it, Danielle," I said, "that makes me think that Chauncey Marquette might be *my* destiny?"

"Cookie?" Danielle asked hopefully.

I pressed a kiss to her hair. "Sure, *mija,* let's go get you a cookie."

I carried her back to the family wing of the house and wished that all desires could be so easily satisfied.

Midnight Destiny

The 6th and final book in the Daughters Of Midnight series is coming in 2020!

ABOUT THE AUTHOR

Ellen Dugan is the award-winning author of over twenty-eight books. Ellen's popular non-fiction titles have been translated into over twelve foreign languages. She branched out successfully into paranormal fiction with her popular *Legacy Of Magick, The Gypsy Chronicles,* and *Daughters Of Midnight* series. Ellen has been featured in USA TODAY'S HEA column. She lives an enchanted life in Missouri tending to her extensive perennial gardens and writing. Please visit her website and blog:

www.ellendugan.com
www.ellendugan.blogspot.com